Begin your Moonlight journey today with a FREE copy of <u>MOONLIGHT FALLS</u>, the first novel in the Thriller and Shamus Award winning series.
Or visit <u>WWW.VINCENTZANDRI.COM</u> to join Vincent's "For your eyes only" newsletter today.

PRAISE FOR VINCENT ZANDRI

"Sensational . . . masterful . . . brilliant."
—New York Post

"(A) chilling tale of obsessive love from Thriller Award–winner Zandri (Moonlight Weeps) . . . Riveting."
—Publishers Weekly

". . . Oh, what a story it is . . . Riveting . . . A terrific old school thriller."
—Booklist "Starred Review"

"I very highly recommend this book . . . It's a great crime drama that is full of action and intense suspense, along with some great twists . . . Vincent Zandri has become a huge name and just keeps pouring out one best seller after another."
—Life in Review

"(The Innocent) is a thriller that has depth and substance, wickedness and compassion."

VINCENT ZANDRI

—The Times-Union (Albany)

"The action never wanes."
—Fort Lauderdale Sun-Sentinel

"Gritty, fast-paced, lyrical and haunting."
—Harlan Coben, New York Times bestselling author of *Six Years*

"Tough, stylish, heartbreaking."
—Don Winslow, New York Times bestselling author of *Savages* and *Cartel.*

"A tightly crafted, smart, disturbing, elegantly crafted complex thriller . . . I dare you to start it and not keep reading."
—MJ Rose, New York Times bestselling author of *Halo Effect* and *Closure*

"A classic slice of raw pulp noir . . ."
—William Landay, New York Times bestselling author of *Defending Jacob*

YOUNG CHASE BAKER
AND THE
CROSS OF THE LAST CRUSADE
A YOUNG CHASE BAKER THRILLER NO. 1

VINCENT ZANDRI

VINCENT ZANDRI

YOUNG CHASE BAKER AND THE CROSS OF THE LAST CRUSADE

For John "Twigs" Weglarz

1963-2017

VINCENT ZANDRI

"O dear Jesus, protect us from the lies, which offend God. Protect us from Satan…"
—*12ᵗʰ Century Knights Templar Battle Prayer*

"I never had any friends later on like the ones I had when I was twelve. Jesus, does anyone?"
—*Stephen King, Stand by Me (adapted from The Body)*

VINCENT ZANDRI

CHAPTER 1

North Albany, NY

Spring, 1979

Why does homework have to suck so bad?

Anyway, I'm plowing through my algebra homework when a noise echoes from downstairs. A loud bang, I should say. It startles me. Sends a cold wave down my spine, makes my stomach go tight, my mouth dry.

I'm home alone.

Pops works till dark in the late spring, and right now he's out of town. He's at least fifty miles away. It's what he calls, making the most of the daylight. He sounds like John Wayne when he says it. John Wayne died a couple years ago, but Dad thinks he's still alive. That a man as big, strong, and take-no-shit tough as John Wayne could never die. Maybe he thinks Elvis is still alive too. I hate Elvis.

Right now, though, I sort of wish John Wayne was standing beside me, because I can hear somebody breaking into the house downstairs. The noise makes my heart pump fast in my chest. It's nothing like when I see Monique Valley, my *sort of* girlfriend, hop onto the school bus in the mornings, her long dark hair freshly washed and combed, her short skirt riding up her smooth, milky thighs. No, this is more like when Mr. Berner, my high school homeroom teacher, sends me to the principal for doing something stupid—like breaking into the high school's basement because rumor had it there's a fully developed fetus stored inside a clear jar filled with embalming fluid.

Berner and me have a love/hate relationship. He loves to hate me. He's accused me of being a thief, a treasure hunter, and even a grave robber in the making. But like I've told him—I can't help myself. If something is old, and I mean like really old, or if there's something mysterious and magical about it, you can count on me to do whatever it takes to dig it up.

That's who I am. That's how I'm wired. You can't change it, any more than you can switch from being right handed to left handed or vice versa. So then, maybe this is a good time to introduce myself. I'm Chase Baker, proud sandhogger's apprentice, future novelist, and yeah, all right I'll admit it—treasure hunter.

Welcome to my world.

Another bang.

Louder this time.

This is disconcerting—one of my favorite new words. Things don't usually go bang downstairs when I'm upstairs doing homework in my bedroom . . . just like Pops wants. Aw, hell. Just like Pops *insists* I do as soon as I get home from school. I guess he knows if I don't do it right away I'll just blow it off for something more exciting like exploring in the farm fields behind the nearby elementary school with my Radio Shack metal detector. Plus, I hate math, and math hates me, so at least we have that established.

But right now, I'm not thinking about math or metal detectors. I'm thinking about the noise downstairs. My heart is in my throat, my pulse is soaring, and my brain is buzzing with adrenalin. I turn around in my desk chair, take a look around the bedroom at the posters of The Beatles and The Who. The world map—covered with thumbtacks indicating the places I've been with Pops on the many sandhogging jobs he's carried out for his university archaeological clients. Egypt, China, Peru . . . Right now, I wish I were on a plane.

But I'm not on a plane.

I'm stuck home all alone while somebody is trying to break in.

Yet another loud bang.

Then a rattling and something dropping hard into the kitchen sink. I don't have to see it first hand to know what's just happened. The screen on the kitchen window above the metal sink has just been busted out.

I slide out my chair, rise up fast, feel the dizziness settle in.

Breathe, Chase, man. Breathe, or you're gonna pass out . . . Imagine how that would look tomorrow in homeroom? Chase Baker passes out while home is robbed!

Chase the self-conscious teen.

Options: Sneak into Dad's bedroom and call the cops. Or, find a baseball bat and face down the intruder like a real man. But I'm only fifteen and five feet five inches tall. I don't even weigh one hundred fifty pounds yet. What if the intruder is a big dude? What if he's armed?

That's when it hits me.

A gun. Dad's got a freakin' gun.

I quietly exit the bedroom, make my way down the narrow hall and into Dad's bedroom. I pull open the drawer in his nightstand and find precisely what I'm looking for.

Dad's Colt .45.

It takes some muscle, but I pull back on the slide and allow a round to enter the chamber. No worries.

Dad has already taught me how to shoot. I can hit a Campbell's Soup can with both eyes open at twenty yards. But I have to keep both hands on the gun, or it will fly back in my face when I fire.

More banging followed by someone shushing someone else.

Oh God, there's two of them. Maybe more.

My body is shaking, knees buckling, throat constricting. I should call the cops. But what if the cops show up and the bad guys get so pissed off they do something horrible to me? The time to call the cops is while they're breaking in, not when they're already breathing down my neck. I have to handle this one on my own. I have to be a man for the first time in my life. Chase the courageous. Or is it Chase the stupid?

YOUNG CHASE BAKER AND THE CROSS OF THE LAST CRUSADE

I tip-toe out of the bedroom back out into the corridor and head for the stairs.

I hear mumbling coming from the kitchen as I begin my descent down the staircase. Mumbling interspersed with little guffaws of laughter. Are these guys drunk? It's not even five o'clock in the afternoon. But then, some of the guys who work on my Pop's job sites sneak away at lunch break to drink beers.

I make out footsteps in the kitchen. They're making their way out of the kitchen and into the vestibule of our two-story, raised ranch home. I continue my descent into the unknown, pistol gripped in both hands, index finger on the trigger, safety off. Two more steps down, and I'll be face to face with them.

"You can do this, Chase," I whisper to myself. "You…can…do…it."

I make out their footsteps and more bursts of laughter.

Whoever broke in has to be drunk or on drugs . . . or both. This is worse than I thought.

I descend the two final steps. That's when I swing the pistol around, take aim.

I shoot.

CHAPTER 2

Here's the deal: I didn't mean to shoot.

My finger was on the trigger and in all the excitement, I kind of pressed down on it. The bullet destroyed the antique mirror hanging on the vestibule wall. The glass shattered into a thousand pieces.

Seven years bad luck. I'm screwed.

The shattering is followed by screams. Two boys my own age are now down on the vestibule floor screaming like girls.

"What the hell, Chase!" one of them belts out.

My friend Dylan Baily, a.k.a. Baily, He raises his head. He's got this look on his round, freckled face like he just crapped himself. The boy lying beside him, his arms covering his head, is John Wilcox, a.k.a. Twigs.

"Baily!" I shout, "Twigs! Are you freakin' crazy? What the hell are you doin'?"

Twigs moves his arms, shifts himself up onto his knees.

He says, "Brainless here thought it would be a real laugh to break into your house and scare the shit out of you." He's breathing heavily. "He thought we'd catch you spanking the monkey or maybe boffing Monique Valley on the couch."

"I don't do that shit," I lie. "Meaning I don't spank the monkey."

"Oh, so that means you and Monique are doing it?" Baily says, voice sprinkled with sarcasm.

I have this sneaking suspicion that Baily has a major crush on Monique and is jealous as hell that she chose me to be her boyfriend. That said, he's always being mean to me about her and mean to her about me. Chalk it up to a teenage love triangle.

"Ummm, sure," I lie once more. "Monique and I get it on all the time."

In my head, I see Monique. She's tall. Taller than me, with long black hair and perky boobs, and a butt so perfect Twigs claims it makes him want to cry. I'd known Monique since second grade and had been carrying a crush on her like pigs carry dirt.

Now, she's my official unofficial girlfriend, which means we sometimes kiss and hold hands if we're lucky enough to be alone. We also talk on the phone six times a day, which I hate. Why don't girls get that boys hate talking on the phone?

Baily stands.

He's taller than most in our class and pretty muscular for a guy who's voice still squeaks when he talks. His hair is thick and red, and it matches his freckled cheeks perfectly. He screams Irish, but if you were to call him Red or Freckles to his face, chances are you'd get a swift wallop to the nose. Baily not only lifts weights, but he takes boxing lessons every Saturday morning at the Free Gym in downtown Albany.

Twigs is a different story.

First of all, his nickname fits him to a T. He's taller than the rest of us, even Baily. But skinny. Gangly according to Pops. He made the JV basketball team just because he's the tallest kid in the class and they needed a center. But he's a spaz when it comes to making baskets. He's got spunk though, and that spunk more than makes up for the muscles that have yet to find their way to his bones.

He likes to use his long arms and fingers like a claw. In other words, when you least expect it, you're liable to feel a big hand grabbing hold of your face followed by a high-pitched, falsetto voice shouting, "The clawwwwwww!!!!" Sometimes "the claw" will be replaced with "The Lariatttt!!!" or simply, "Reachhingggg!!!" But the point is the same. To catch you by surprise and, if at all possible, to make you crap yourself. The three of us might be tighter than Twig's pearl white BVDs, but we love to scare the hell out of one another. Which explains their breaking into my house and my fucking up by shooting out Pops' antique mirror.

And speaking of Pops, my amigos must have somehow figured out he wasn't home, because never in a million years would they be stupid or fearless enough to attempt a break-in when he was guarding the castle. Pops might not be the tallest dude in the world, but he can bench press three-fifteen eight times. He owns guns, and he don't take no shit (Remember the John Wayne thing).

"Where'd you get the fucking hand cannon, dude?" Baily asks. "Your old man know you have that?"

"It's his pistol, duh," I say, staring into the destroyed mirror. "You're lucky he's not home, or you'd both be full of holes."

"His Jeep is gone," Baily explains.

I see my face reflected a million times in the scattered triangles of cracked glass. My too-freakin'-thick black hair, my round face, the red blemish from a pimple I popped on my left cheek last night, the hint of sporadic facial hair creeping in. I would never say this to the others, but I'm hoping to grow a mustache like Tom Selleck by this time next year. Tom Selleck is the star of that show, Magnum PI. He's badass.

Then, a wide, sweaty, smelly hand suddenly plants on my face.

"The clawwwwwwww!!!!"

The hand hooks onto my chin and jaw pulling me completely around.

"Fuck you, Twigs!" I shout.

But the two of them are laughing so hard they might piss their Levis.

"Okay," I say when the hand is removed. "So, what the hell is the deal? What's so important you gotta break into my house?"

I head into the kitchen, set the .45 onto the counter, go to the kitchen sink. Hopping up onto the counter, I replace the screen, then jump back down to the floor. At least I won't get chewed out for that.

"You know that rich old dude, Mr. Menands, lives in that old creepy mansion down by Montgomery Ward?" Baily explains, his blue eyes wide inside his red face. "Well, he croaked, and they buried him just this morning."

He grabs the pistol, aims it out the window, makes shooting sounds with his mouth. I take the gun slowly out of his hand, set it back down on the counter.

"That's not a toy, asshole," I explain, eyes wide. Then, "And why should I give a crap about that mean old bastard, Menands?"

Baily raises his hands, makes fists, starts jabbing at me. I duck left and land one on his sternum.

"Asshole," he says. He grabs my head in a headlock, knuckles my skull. "Noogy!"

He laughs, releases me, and I start chasing him around the kitchen. Twigs is oblivious while he inspects the refrigerator, emerges with a piece of cheese pizza left over from last night's supper. If there's one thing Twigs can do, it's eat. Yet, the more he eats, the more weight he seems to drop. He's a freak of nature.

The phone rings.

I stop my pursuit of Baily and take a breath.

"There's Make-Me-Moan-Monique!" Baily teases while making kissy lips. "What's that, like the tenth time she's called you today?" Then, in mock Monique voice. "Oh, I soooo need to talk it up with my Chase Baker boy. I sooooo need him to touch me all over . . . make me moan, Chase."

I feel my face flush red.

"Everybody shut up," I insist. "That could be the old man."

"What's he, like . . . forty now?" Twigs says, a half a slice of cold pizza stuffed in his cheeks. "We gotta start calling him grandpa. Grandpa Baker."

I pick up the wall-mounted phone, put it to my ear.

"Hello!" I bark.

"How come you don't say 'Baker residence,' like I asked?" the voice questions.

I was right. It's the old man.

"What's up, Pops?" I say, trying to put a little pep in my voice. "Just hanging out doing my math homework. You know, nose to the grindstone and all that." I laugh and hope it sounds convincing.

The connection goes quiet. Or, that's not entirely right. More like Pops stops speaking and the silence fills with the familiar sounds of an excavation site. Diesel-powered tractors and the creaky, metal-on-metal sound of a backhoe digging something up. I've grown up with my Pop's sandhogging business, sometimes spending entire days on job sites. I don't have my mom anymore, so up until very recently, Pops had no choice but to take me everywhere. Something we both sort of enjoyed.

"Chase," he says after a beat, "whenever you, of all people, volunteer the state of your homework on a no-school day and do so with a chipper voice, I know damn well you're up to no good. So, what'd you break this time? Or did you dig something up you weren't supposed to?"

A start in my ticker. I picture the broken mirror, and the glass that's, at present, strewn all over the vestibule floor.

"Ummm, nope. Nothing," I lie. Then, trying to change the subject. "So, what's up, Pops? Whaddaya wanna do for supper? How about we hit up the Pizza Hut?"

"That's the thing, kid," he says. "I won't be home for dinner. In fact, I probably won't get home 'till after you've gone to bed. We uncovered a whole bunch of graves dating back to the slave trade days, and these university archaeologists are pissing themselves they're so excited. You know the way they get."

My heart goes from startled to all aflutter. I get the house to myself all night. I picture my Pops with the office trailer phone pressed to his ear. He's a short, stocky guy, sort of like me, but with a trim black beard plus salt and pepper hair. He wears black horned rim glasses, and he lives in blue jeans, a pair of worn brown Chippewa work boots that are older than I am, and a tan button-down work shirt, both pockets no doubt stuffed with packing slips, cash, cigarettes, maps, and who knows what else. The keys to his Jeep CJ will be hanging from his leather belt by means of a carabineer purchased in the Adirondacks at a rock-climbing-slash-hiking-slash-fly fishing store called The Mountaineer.

"Oh, it's okay, Pops," I say. "There's Spaghetti-Os in the cabinet and plenty of milk. Some leftover pizza too." My eyes focus in on Twigs. He's on his second slice, and he's shaking his head while running an index finger across his throat, telling me

the pizza is, in fact, history. "Yup, plenty of pizza.
I'll be fine, Pops."

"Okay, kid, you sure?" the old man begs. "Because,
I can figure out a way to get home on time while
Tommy Pats runs the show."

Tommy Patton, or Tommy Pats, is my Pops' right-
hand man. He's older than my dad. Like, older than
the hills World War II vet old. A little wiry guy who
works the cemetery excavating graves on his off
hours. He lives and breathes for dirt.

"That won't be necessary, Pops," I insist. "Got a
shitload—errrrr oops—a boatload of homework to
do. I'll be okay."

He hesitates again like he doesn't trust me and my
homework comments. I'd better cool them off or

he'll hang up, get in his Jeep, and head home right now.

"Okay then, Son," he says. "Gotta go. I'll check in with you later, see how you're doing. Make sure you eat some vegetables and lock the doors, you hear me?"

"Got it, Pops. See ya later."

He hangs up. Suddenly, I feel like a prison inmate who's just been granted a reprieve from the electric chair. I also feel myself smiling ear to ear. Tonight, it's great to be Chase Baker.

"What's up?" Twigs inquires. He's drinking milk from right out of the carton.

"Jeeze, don't drink me dry, asshole."

He sets the carton down on the counter beside the Colt, wipes his mouth with the back of his hand.

"Easy, Chase," he says with a smile. "Easyyyyyyyy now." He picks the carton back up, shakes it so that I can make out the few droplets left inside it. "You need more milk, too."

"Listen," I say. "What's going on? What's with this dead Menands guy?"

"Talk to Baily about that one," Twigs insists. "It's all his brilliant idea."

I head out of the kitchen, through the dining room with its antique wood table and walls covered in cherry wood paneling, and into the living room. Well, it's not much of living room since Pops has turned it into an office-slash-study. There are floor-to-ceiling bookshelves covering the three walls that don't have windows. The shelves not only hold thousands of books, but dozens of old relics Pops has dug up over the years in some pretty exotic locations. There are half-moon-shaped daggers from Morocco, a doll made of Lama wool from Peru, ceramic bowls from China, a black mini Sphynx from Cairo, and a bunch of other stuff that could probably fill up a small museum.

Long wood tables are covered with maps of the world, and a gun rack mounted to the wall close to the far corner holds a couple of shotguns, two bolt action rifles, and even a Tommy Gun from World War II. There are also file cabinets, bins filled with rolled up blueprints, schematics, maps of foreign lands, and more junk than you can swing an ancient Egyptian dagger at. If I didn't know this was my home, I might confuse the place for Howard

YOUNG CHASE BAKER AND THE CROSS OF THE LAST CRUSADE

Carter's private office. For anyone not up on their Egyptology, Howard Carter was the dude who discovered King Tut's tomb.

Baily has his face stuffed in a book.

"This is it," he says, planting the tip of his finger on a picture displayed in the volume.

"What are you talking about?" I ask.

Twigs enters the room.

"I'm starving," he says. "Let's go get some food."

"The Crusader Cross," Baily says. "Or, what's also known in some circles as the Cross of the Last Crusade. Catchy, ain't it?"

Together, Twigs and I gaze at the picture of the cross. It is pretty incredible if I must say so. Even though it's only a color photo, it still sort of takes your breath away. But then, like I said, I'm a sucker for this kind of ancient treasure thing.

"Holy crap," Twigs says, equally impressed.

"That's solid gold there, brothers," Baily says, his enthusiasm showing in his now blood red cheeks. "And those stones stuck in the center? Rubies and sapphires."

"*Embedded* in the center," I say, correcting him.

"Whatever, Baker," he says. "Don't be a dick. You're not a writer yet. The point is that this cross is ours, tonight."

I start laughing.

"And what are we supposed to do, fly to Paris and be back for school tomorrow?"

"No duh," Baily says, closing the book hard. "That cross is closer than you think, nitwit."

"How close?" Twigs asks in his nasally high-pitched voice.

"It's a mile down the road in the Albany Rural Cemetery," Baily replies with a grin on his face. "It's six feet under."

"Six feet under, as in buried in a grave," I say like I'm asking a question with an obvious answer.

"Baker," Baily says. "You're the digger. Go grab us some shovels."

VINCENT ZANDRI

CHAPTER 3

In my head, I'm picturing the cross. Picturing myself touching it. Picturing it doing its magic. I'll say it again: I'm a total sucker for ancient relics, but what Baily is talking about is nothing short of grave robbing, and I tell him exactly that.

"The dude's dead," Baily argues. "What the hell is he gonna do with a cross worth millions of bucks?"

"Doesn't matter what the cross is worth, Baily," I say. "It belongs in a museum."

"Then you agree it should be excavated," Twigs says. "By that logic, anyway."

They both have me stumped for a second. If this guy, Menands, did, in fact, bury the cross along with his old corpse then it only makes sense that it be dug back up and handed over to the authorities in France or, at the very least, delivered to the Albany Institute of History and Art down on State Street in the city. My Pops is a member of their board, and they'll see to it that the cross is well taken care of. Plus, if I were to deliver it to them, I would look like the adventurous hero. Chase the dreamer.

"Remind me who this guy, Menands, was again," I insist. "I just remember him as the rich old mean guy who lived in that haunted mansion on the other side of town."

"Pierre Menands," Baily says. "The little North Albany Village is named after him. He was born in Paris in like the 1880s and moved here just before the war. The second one with Hitler and all those goose-stepping assholes."

Twigs reaches out, claws Baily's face.

"It's the goose step!" he barks in a voice that could break a wine glass.

"Cut it out, ass wipe," Baily spits. Then, shaking his head. "Now, where was I?"

"World War II, Paris, Menands," I remind him.

"Oh yeah," he says. "So, back in the 1940s, Menands is like filthy rich, and apparently he's got this collection of art and ancient relics that's supposed to be priceless and world famous. He knows the Germans are gonna snatch it all up now that they've invaded Paris, so what's he do?"

"He moves it out," Twigs sings to the tune of that new Billy Joel song, *Moving Out*. Twigs loves rock 'n roll. He's got tons of albums, a big ass stereo system with huge speakers, and has already been to like a hundred concerts up in Saratoga Springs with his big sister.

"Exactamundo," Baily says. "Menands and his collection board a boat that takes them across the Atlantic. They move to quiet, suburban North Albany. He buys up the Montgomery Ward superstore, establishes the Village of Menands, and he gets even richer."

"He was creepy," Twigs adds.

"Well," Baily goes on, "legend has it that as soon as he took possession of the Cross of the Last Crusade, it placed a curse on him. He became old before his years, and he never married or had kids. He lived in that house alone, except for one man who remained loyal to him until the end. That man, I'm told, placed the cross and some other riches inside Menands' casket, according to the old bastard's explicit instructions."

"How do you know all this stuff?" I ask. "You only get Cs in history."

"My mother works with some people in the know at the Montgomery Ward department store. They say he took the cross with him into the eternity. You know, the great beyond."

I turn, step out into the vestibule, the glass of the broken mirror crunching under my feet.

What if Baily is right? What if the Cross of the Last Crusade really is newly buried along with Pierre Menands' rotting corpse? What would Pops say? I know exactly what he'd say: *Is it right that an artifact of such historical significance be buried forever just because one man wants it that way? One very cranky, now dead, old man?*

I turn back to Baily.

"And what exactly is the history behind the cross?" I ask.

He finger taps the old leather-bound book, his excitement-filled red face lit up like a lightbulb.

"According to ancient legend," he says, "the cross was snatched up by the French Knights Templar warrior, Henry 'Hotspur' Percy during one of the Crusades in Jerusalem in the eleven hundreds. He brought it back to Paris for the King who then ordered it to be placed on the altar of the newly constructed Notre-Dame cathedral where it remained for many years until it was snatched up once more by robbers and disappeared."

"Only to show back up in the Menands collection centuries later," I add. "Go figure." Then, me smiling. "Jeeze, Baily, I gotta hand it to ya. For a high school screw up, you really know your shit."

"When it comes to making dough." He smiles smugly, raising his eyebrows up and down.

Twigs crosses his arms over his chest and purses his lips.

"This whole thing stinks, you ask me," he says.

"We get caught digging up a grave we'll go to jail. Now, can we go? I'm starving. We can stop off at McDonald's on the way. Or better yet, Charlie's Hot Dogs."

"You gotta stop eating that crap," Baily says. "It'll make you fat, pal."

Baily and I look the too thin Twigs up and down.

"Or on the other hand," Baily goes on, "maybe not."

Pop's study goes quiet for a beat until Twigs thrusts out his right hand and grabs Baily's face.

"Reachhhhhinngggggggg!" he shrieks. Then, while releasing Baily, "Since I'm the only one with a driver's license, I get to say where we eat and where we don't eat."

"Yeah, yeah, yeah," Baily says, rubbing the life back into cheeks. "One thing's for sure, we gotta wait till dark anyway. We can't just go digging up a dead dude while the sun's still out. You gotta do it under the cover of darkness."

"I guess that's where I come in," I say.

Baily smiles. "Gee, ya think?"

"Okay," I say. "I'll supply the tools, but if we do this, we must agree on one thing."

"What's that, homo?" Baily asks.

"That if and when we get our hands on the cross, we turn it over to a museum."

Baily scrunches his face.

"Oh, come on, Chase," he barks. "You know how much money we can get for it?"

"Oh, really?" I say. "And who exactly are we gonna sell it to? Vito Corleone?" I shake my head and jab him in the chest. "You don't have a choice, Beetle Baily. It's either the museum, or you find some other asshole to do your digging."

More silence for a few beats.

Then Baily assumes a sourpuss glare. He says, "I guess you got a point. Not like we know how to hock it on the black market anyway." But then his frown turns upside down. "Hey, I can betcha, however, that the museum will give us a nice reward for the famous golden cross."

All three of us work up smiles.

"Now you're talking, Baily," I say. "We're gonna be rich *and* well respected."

"And famous," Baily says.

I pat him on the shoulders with both hands.

"That's the spirit, buddy."

"Jesus, pretty soon you guys will be making out," Twigs insists. "Let's go. I don't get something to eat soon, I'm gonna pass out."

VINCENT ZANDRI

CHAPTER 4

We pile into Twig's late dad's green Chevy Suburban—Twigs behind the wheel, Baily in the shotgun seat, and me, with the shorter legs, always relegated to the back seat. When I ask them both about how they expect to get away with spending the night digging up Menands' grave, they insist they're in the clear.

"My mom's working the night shift at the restaurant," Baily says. "She locks up. Won't be home until after two. My dad's in Saudi Arabia managing a construction project."

We turn to Twigs who is clearly scoping out the many fast food restaurants that flank the North Albany road.

"Hey, my mom is probably already asleep," he says. "You both know about my dad."

Twigs' dad died of a heart attack a couple of years back. Nice guy who used to drive us to basketball practice back when we were still in junior high, he got up one morning, put on his work boots and dropped dead. It was the damnedest thing. Since then, Twigs has sort of been the very young man of the family, taking care of the household chores, plus keeping up the routine maintenance on both his old man's Suburban and his mother's Cadillac. Between that, school, sports, and messing around with Baily and me, it's a wonder he has time to sleep.

It was settled. We don't actually come out and say it, but it's understood that we're officially going after the Cross of the Last Crusade as soon as it gets dark, which should be within the hour.

Without warning, Twigs pulls into Charlie's Hot Dogs, pulls around to the take-out window. Since we all have to eat, he orders on our behalf, then makes each of us cough up two bucks a piece. Five minutes later, we're all seated around a picnic table outside the restaurant, feasting on half a dozen hotdogs per person smothered with the works. Charlie's specializes in mini-hot dogs—about three inches long and they go "pop" in your mouth when you bite into them. The tangy, spicy red sauce they douse them in, along with chopped onions and relish, creates a flavor explosion for your taste buds. A large Coke and a large order of fries to go with them, and you're in heaven on Earth.

"Let's talk logistics," Baily says as he grabs his third dog. "What are you planning on using to dig up the Menands coffin?"

I munch down on one of my hotdogs. You can kill one single dog with two bites.

"Shovels and pickaxes," I say. "Why?"

"You've obviously never dug up a fresh grave before, sandhogger," Baily says, smiling slyly. "Oh, or am I being a dick again?"

"He's right, brother Chase," Twigs says. His tray is already clean. I can tell by the pensive look on his face, he's contemplating buying another half dozen. He adds, "We use shovels we'll be there all night. Plus, what do we do when we get down to the coffin? The casket will likely be stored inside a concrete vault, just like my dad is. You know, so it's preserved for all eternity, like it really matters at this point." He looks at Baily's hot dog tray. "You gonna eat that last one, Freckles?"

"Keep it up twat-face-Twigs," Baily barks, annoyed. Then, nodding his head over his shoulder. "Go ahead, knock yourself out. Those things are already giving me heartburn."

"Reachhhinggggggg," Twigs says, snatching up the hotdog and stuffing it in his mouth before Baily changes his mind. "You shouldn't be getting heartburn. You're too young for that. You already sound like my Uncle Jim, works at the auto parts store. He drinks Maalox for breakfast."

"Thanks," Baily says. "I'll make a note of that." Refocusing on me. "Twigs is right. We need some serious excavating power, we're gonna get at that cross in a reasonable amount of time."

"What's a reasonable amount of time?" I ask, digging into my fourth hotdog.

"Like a half hour duh," Baily says. "The longer we take, the better chance we got of being nailed by the cops. At least in my opinion."

I lock eyes with Baily.

"Whatttttt?" he poses, wide-eyed.

"Whaddaya wanna be when you grow up?" I ask.

He gives me a smirk. "Why you asking me that?"

"Because I have a feeling you're either gonna be a real good thief or one hell of a politician," I state.

He keeps staring at me, but after a few beats, cracks a smile.

"You really think so?" he says.

"Judging by the way you think, Beetle Baily," I say.

"Yeah," Twigs chimes in, picking at his teeth with a toothpick. "You sound like you've got experience in the grave robbing business, Baily man."

Baily nods and says, "Despite my humble grades, I happen to read a lot. You imbeciles should try it some time." Then, standing. "It's getting dark. We gotta move."

I stand, and at the same time, hand over my last two Charlie's hotdogs to Twigs.

"More reachingggggg," he sings, grabbing both at once.

"So, what's it gonna be, Baker?" Baily pushes. "Shovels and pickaxes followed by jail? Or can you use all the powers at your disposal to access the heavy machinery?"

"You asking me to steal my Pop's backhoe, Baily?"

"Borrow, is more like it," he smiles.

I feel my insides go south. Because they're right, of course. We need a backhoe or no ancient cross.

"You guys better hope my old man doesn't decide to come home early," I say, turning for the Suburban.

YOUNG CHASE BAKER AND THE CROSS OF THE LAST CRUSADE

"Don't you worry," Baily adds. "We'll get it to the cemetery and back again all within a half hour. He won't even know it's been missing."

"Good," I say. "Because he hates surprises. Especially when they come from me."

A flesh and blood claw wraps entirely around my face, pulling me backward.

"The larriattttttttttttt!!!" Twigs shouts. "Surprise!"

VINCENT ZANDRI

CHAPTER 5

Soon as we get back to my house, I head into the vestibule and clean up the shattered mirror. When I'm done, I stare at the nickel-sized hole in the wall and try to figure out how to repair it. I give up after a few seconds because I know there's nothing I can do. Instead, I go to Pop's desk and look through the keyring he keeps in the top drawer. At least two dozen keys are stored on the ring, including the extra key to the CAT backhoe parked in the backyard, along with a couple of compressors, a bulldozer, a ditch witch, and some core drills. I pull the key off the ring, stuff it into my jeans pocket.

"What now?" I pose to my amigos.

"Your dad got anything that might make us look official?" Baily asks.

He's seated up on the counter in the kitchen. Twigs, as usual, has his face in the fridge. I'm standing by the sink, one eye on the yard in back where dad's sandhogging and excavating equipment is stored under a protective spotlight, the other on the guys.

"Official?" I question.

"Jeeze, you're dumb," Baily goes on, rolling his blue eyes. "Some sort of clothing or overalls to make us look like we're official cemetery employees, just in case a cop drives past or something like that."

Twigs closes the fridge door. He's got a slice of chocolate cake in his hand.

"Baily's got a point," he offers. "We need flashlights too, so we can see our way in the dark." Then, bringing the cake up to his mouth. "How old is this cake anyway?"

Before I can inform him that it's at least a month old and probably spotted with green mold, he's already chomping down on it.

"We should find all that stuff in the work shed out back," I say.

Baily slides off the counter, the soles of his Converse high tops landing hard on the yellow linoleum. "Times a wastin'," he says.

The phone rings.

I look at Baily, then Twigs. They're looking back at me.

"That ring has got Monique's name all over it," Baily snipes.

"She's got the lariottttt around your neck," Twigs says.

In my head, I see Monique on the phone in her father's den, her long black hair veiling her sweet face. *Crap,* I whisper inside my head.

I lead my three amigos out the back door and into the yard while the phone rings off the hook.

The yard behind the house is big and wide. Maybe an acre of land surrounded by a chain link fence that's accessed by a gate that manually swings open and closed. There's no padlock on the gate since this is a quiet suburban neighborhood with very little crime. The yard contains the equipment I've already mentioned plus a shed that doubles as a machine garage where the old man and Tommy Pats work on repairs and routine maintenance. An expansive room beside the garage is used for storage of small hand tools and other equipment like oil cans, chains, ropes, shovels, pickaxes, and yup— flashlights. I'm just hoping the batteries are fresh.

The guys follow me into the storage room. I flip up the wall-mounted switch, and the room lights up like a Brezhnev USSR nuclear test blast from the bright overheads. The square, windowless room has floor-to-ceiling metal racks pressed against the walls. The racks are filled with all sorts of junk, some of it has collected a thick coat of dust. Just

like his collection of rare antiquities, Pops can't
seem to work up the courage to toss anything out.

*"Today's junk is tomorrow's treasure, Son," he
likes to say.*

"That's what we need right there," Baily says,
pointing at one of the racks to our right-hand side
where a dozen or more sets of overalls are hanging
by hangers. The shelves behind the overalls house
hardhats, goggles, ear protectors, and gloves.

"The motherload," Baily adds, a smile on his face.
"Why didn't you speak up before, Baker? Jeeze
Louise. We got everything we need right here to
conceal ourselves, just like a real adventure movie.
Once we dress up in this shit, nobody will ever
guess how old we are."

. . . a real adventure movie . . .

I'm beginning to think that's what this is all about for Dylan Baily. A real-life adventure movie starring John Wayne or Sean Connery. Chase the suspicious.

"I guess when you live with this stuff, you don't really pay it any attention," I say.

"Let's get dressed, boys," Twigs says, making his way for the rack. "Hope you got my size, brother Chase. Extra long."

"Like my Dick Johnson." Baily smiles.

"Tiny Dick Johnson," Twigs says, making little pretend pinchers with his index finger and thumb.

Moments later, we no longer resemble teenage boys. Instead, we're wearing gray overalls which, in my case anyway, are a couple sizes too big in the legs and arms. But combined with the white hardhats, work gloves, and goggles, create the impression of three hard-core adult workers. Adult being the key word here.

"What's left on the prep list?" Twigs asks, his gloved hand now chasing after Baily's face, making his goggles go crooked.

"Cut that shit out, Twigs," Baily barks, straightening his goggles and hardhat. "I'm trying to think."

"So, that explains the smoke coming out of your ears," Twigs says.

"Fell off my freakin' dinosaur last time I heard that one, asshole," Baily snaps.

"There is one thing we're forgetting," I point out.

The two go still, lock eyes on mine.

"What?" they pose in unison.

"The location of the Menands grave."

"The Albany Rural Cemetery is pretty freakin' massive," Twigs says. "Like Wanda Wollowinski's ass."

Baily snorts and laughs at the mention of our long red-haired classmate with the funny name and ummm . . . major league booty that isn't altogether as unattractive as Twigs pretends. But then, Twigs prefers girls who are as skinny as he is, which pretty much means he's into skeletons or girls with serious eating disorders.

"I think I know where we'll find it," I say.

"Where, Baker?" Baily pleads. "In your

bungholio?"

"Close," I say. "In the Times Union Newspaper."

CHAPTER 6

We head back into the house. I go to Dad's desk in the living room and pull out the day's newspaper from under his pile of mail. I spread it open on the desk.

"I saw this picture this morning on the front page," I say. "I didn't think a whole hell of a lot about it until just now."

We gather around Dad's desk, focus on the newspaper's front page. Baily reads the headline aloud.

"Menands Mourned," he recites. "I always took him for a cranky stingy old bastard. Who would ever miss somebody like that?"

"He gave a lot of money to the community," Twigs points out. "Remember, he started the village of Menands, for Christs sakes. Give a dead guy a little credit."

"That he did, Twigs," I say. "Dude, employed a lot of people at Montgomery Ward, including your mom, Baily. So, it's no wonder he'll be missed. By the grownups anyway."

"Okay, so what are we looking at?" Baily presses.

Below the headline is a big black and white photo of the graveside funeral service at the Albany Rural Cemetery. The big black casket is set out on top of a platform that's draped with what looks like a black bed sheet. A group of mourners dressed in black surround it. They're all holding roses in their hands. Directly beside the casket is a rectangular hole in the ground, where Mr. Menands will presumably spend all of eternity. That is until the worms get to him. There's a tent set up over the open grave in case it rains, I guess.

"Okay, that tree is one landmark," I say, using my index finger like a pointer, pressing it down on the massive old oak tree that takes up a whole lot of the picture's left side.

"You know how many trees are in that cemetery?" Baily comments. "Like, thousands. Lots of old oaks too. The place has got to be twenty square miles with long winding roads, hills, streams, and even a creepy crematorium, man. You're reaching if you think that's our benchmark."

I know what's coming even before Twigs reaches out, claws my face with his gloved hand.

"Reachinggggggg!" he squeals.

Like Baily before me, my goggles go all screwy, and I'm forced to readjust them.

"Stop that shit already," I say. "Even with gloves on, your hands smell like Charlie's Hot Dogs, you bag of bones."

"I resent that," he says with a smile.

"Okay, agreed," I state, refocused on the picture. "That tree isn't much of a benchmark. But if we look close enough, we just might be able to find—" My voice trails off.

"Find what, Baker?" Twigs asks.

"That's it," I say.

I'm now pointing to a monument that's barely captured in the shot. It's unique in that it's a very tall monument topped off with the Celtic cross. At its base is a stone chamber for housing the casket, instead of it being buried six feet under like most dead folks. It's a special monument that will one day be home to the Mayor of Albany. Dude called Erastus Corning. He's been mayor for something like forty years already, and he doesn't show any signs of dying soon. But then, what the hell do I know? I'm just a kid.

Anyway, his monument is famous enough that Pops pointed it out to me once when we were out for one of his long "educational ghost tours" at some historic cemetery that's also home to US President

Chester Arthur, whoever the hell he was.

"What is it, Baker?" Baily pushes.

"You see that monument there?"

Baily scrunches his eyes. So does Twigs.

"What monument?" Twigs asks.

"It's there. Trust me," I say. "My dad gave me an

entire ten minute lecture on it once. It belongs to the

mayor of Albany."

"The Mayor's still alive, duh," Baily says.

"I know he's alive, douche," I retort. "But one day

he won't be, and when that happens, that monument

will become his new apartment."

"Little more cramped than the last one," Twigs

jokes with a snort.

"The point being," I go on, "I know precisely where Menands' grave is located based on the location of that monument."

Baily smiles.

"I get it," he says. "It's just like the Hardy Boys. This picture is our treasure map, and that monument is the X. And X—"

Twigs plants his claw on Baily's face once more, squeezes his red cheeks.

"—X marks the spot, Freckles!!!" he shouts.

VINCENT ZANDRI

CHAPTER 7

I tear the photograph from the newspaper, shove it into the side pocket on my overalls. I pull the key to the backhoe from the same pocket, yank my goggles down over my eyes, and adjust the hardhat so it fits just right. Heart pumping in my chest, I'm ready to roll. That's when the phone rings.

"Aww Jeeze," Baily says like Archie Bunker from his favorite boob tube show, *All in the Family*. "There she is again."

"Whipped," Twigs sings under his breath. "Pussy . . . whipped . . . Baker man."

"Listen," I say. "It won't take me a second. Besides, it could be the old man making a check on me."

But in my heart of hearts, I know it isn't the old man. As much as he loves me, like both a mother *and* a father, there's one thing my pops taught me that so many other parents don't teach their kids. Self-reliance. I'm not saying my old man is hands-off, here's-the-cable-TV-box-there's-food-in-the-fridge-don't-forget-to-lock-up-before-bed kind of parent. I'm saying he trusts me to get the things done that I'm supposed to get done and to take care of myself in his absence, which seems to be occurring more and more these days now that his services are in demand not only from archaeologists housed at the New York State universities but also universities around the world.

He also expects me to do the right thing when he isn't around which makes me feel weird if not downright anxious over what we were about to pull off in the Albany Rural Cemetery. What I'm saying is, I know it's totally wrong in the eyes of both God and the law to be digging up a dead body. And in my gut, I know it's even more wrong to be stealing away a cross that bears huge historical significance for the rest of eternity. But it belongs in a museum, and that's where I intend to deliver it. So what if I end up breaking a few rules and laws along the way. In the end, Pops will be proud that I took the initiative. That I relied on myself and my own smarts to get it done. That I did the mature thing. The right thing.

I pick up the phone.

"Hello."

"There you are," Monique Valley coos. "I've been calling and calling, cutie."

Cutie. Why did she have to say cutie? It always turns me into a puddle of useless Silly Putty when she calls me cutie. I see her in my head. Beautiful Monique, all alone, sitting on her portly, bald, lawyer dad's desk inside his office, his phone extension pressed to her ear, her legs long and smooth, the tips of her toes barely touching the floor. Maybe she's wearing a Nike t-shirt or one of her Jackson Browne t-shirts with cut-off jeans and white Keds sneakers. I imagine her sweet long dark hair and her fingers combing it back over her head, so it doesn't keep falling into her eyes. Chase the always in love.

"Sorry, Monique," I say. "The guys are here. We've been, ummm, busy."

"Usually all you guys do is sit around and eat and listen to tunes in Twigs' basement. Or shoot hoops in his driveway."

"We're at my house," I say, trying to think quick. "We're working on a project for school."

"Really?" she says, chipper as all hell. "My parents are up at the lake house for the long weekend. They left a day early."

"They left you alone?"

"They trust me silly. I'm a girl. And girls are way more mature than boys."

Oh great, I think. *A dead old man newly buried, an ancient cross made of solid gold worth hundreds of*

millions of dollars buried along with him, and all us
kids on the loose. The recipe for a perfect storm of
mega trouble.

"That's true," I say. "Pops always said girls are
more mature than boys. I guess I believe him."

"Sooooo," she says, like a question.

Baily enters the kitchen. He puckers his lips, brings
his hand to his mouth, blows me a kiss. I about-
face. Twigs is standing there. He's about to give me
the claw.

"So what, Monique?" I say.

"Are you gonna invite me over, silly?"

Monique lives in the neighborhood behind mine. A
dwelling separated by a small state park that
contains an even smaller lake appropriately called,

Little's Lake. It's an easy bike ride, or if you're on foot, you can cut through the trails. Either way, it only takes five minutes to get to my house from her house.

"Invite you over?" I repeat, so the other guys hear me.

Baily bites down on his bottom lip. He does that thing again where he runs his index finger across his neck like I'm supposed to be scared or something.

"No . . . chicks!" he mouths.

"Bite me," I mouth back while flipping him off.

I glance at Twigs. He's gesturing at me with his claw outstretched. Like he's *reaching* but can't quite get to me. When translated, the gesture also means, no chicks.

"You there . . . cutie?" Monique chimes in.

Oh God, why does she have to say it like that? So sweet and gentle?

"I'm here," I say. "Look, it's sort of a boy's night if you know what I mean. And we're just working on a school thing, so it'll be boring, Monique."

A pause in the connection. I can hear her breathing. In my head, I see her chest filling out her t-shirt while she breathes. Why does life have to be so hard?

"Chase," she says. "Are you blowing me off?"

"No, Monique," I say. "Not at all. It's just that we have this shit to do, and—"

YOUNG CHASE BAKER AND THE CROSS OF THE LAST CRUSADE

"—I'll be in the way, is that it?" she challenges.

"No, that's not how I was gonna put it." My head's spinning. If this is what it's like to be married, I already want a divorce.

"But like, that's what you *meant*," she accuses.

Now, in my head, Monique's no longer sitting casually at her dad's desk, but instead, standing straight and stiff, her body trembling mad. She's French, and when she gets mad, even my grandmother can feel it. And my grandmother is dead.

"Well, you listen to me, Chase Baker," she barks. "This is it. If you'd rather be with your *friends,* that's perfectly fine by me. But then don't expect *me* to be here for *you* whenever you *want*. Have a nice night, asshole."

She hangs up. So hard it hurts my ear.

I hang up, my body feeling like the crap's just been kicked out of it. If I were an adult, I think this is the time where I'd pour a drink and smoke a cigarette.

"So, how'd that go, Brother Chase?" Twigs asks. "Still glad you got a girlfriend?"

"Told you not to pick up the phone, dummy," Baily says, his arms crossed over his chest. But my guess is, he'd jump at the chance to be getting phone calls from Monique Valley, the best-looking girl in our class.

We're standing in the kitchen in our overalls, goggles, and hard hats, looking like Devo, and all I want to do is cry.

"Can we just go get that cross, already?" I say.

"Waitin' on you, buddy," Baily says.

"Back door," I say. "Everybody on the backhoe."

My two amigos turn, head for the back door that leads out into the yard. I follow. But then, at the last second, I turn back around, go into the kitchen, grab the .45 off the counter. I run it upstairs, place it back into dad's bedside drawer where it belongs.

"Hey," I say to myself. "Pops will never know the difference."

But then considering the busted antique mirror and the bullet hole in the wall, it's just wishful thinking.

VINCENT ZANDRI

CHAPTER 8

I hop up onto the backhoe, slip into the cockpit, take my seat behind the wheel, and fire her up. Since the cockpit is way too small for more than one dude at a time, the others ride on the sideboards and hang on for dear life while I pull out of the shed, drive along the dirt two-track to the gate.

"Somebody get the gate," I bark when we come to it.

"Reachhhinggg," Twigs says, jumping off, making his way to the unlocked gate and opening it wide.

I pull through the gate, and he jumps back up onto the runner. Turning the headlights on, I pull the digging machine out onto the road. It bucks and rocks as we head in the direction of the cemetery. It's dark out, but it's still pretty early, which means there are plenty of cars on the road. Lots of people are straining their necks to get a look at us. What I'm banking on is that between our work overalls and my, more or less, professional handling of the backhoe, we fit the bill of a nighttime excavating crew.

Here's what I'm also hoping: that we don't run into a cop.

It's the longest mile of my life.

The machine bobs to and fro like we're riding an unstable boat on a choppy sea. The big front bucket dips while the dinosaur-like rear shovel rises violently up only to see-saw the other way. The big diesel engine revs and spits while the shovels we brought along clatter inside the cab. We can't help but attract attention on the road. People driving past rubberneck at us like we're an accident waiting to happen. Finally, we arrive at the gates to the Albany Rural Cemetery. It's the oldest cemetery in Albany County, according to Pops anyway. It's first body was laid to rest all the way back in 1842 on April Fool's Day. A fact that tickles the old man to death.

I pull up to the open gates, come to a stop.

The cemetery before us is dark and foreboding. Trees and thick foliage cover a landscape of old headstones, and mausoleums. They add a weird thickness to the darkness. For a second or two, I can't help but feel like I'm caught up in a rerun of that old Dark Shadows TV show Pops forbade me to watch when I was really little. In any case, it's as if we're about to enter a different dimension altogether—a place where the lines between the living and dead are not so clearly defined.

"Okay, gentlemen," I say from the cockpit, my hands gripping the steering wheel. "No going back from here."

I'm flanked by my best friends. Under normal circumstances, they are happy-go-lucky—if not silly—dudes. We have fun together. We rarely fight. Well, Baily gave me a black eye once over a girl. But we made up, and at the same time, forgot about the girl. In some ways, we can't live without one another. There have even been times I've thought about maybe buying a house with these guys when we're all grown up. It would be fun. Maybe we'll even travel the world together and go on the hunt for buried treasure as a team.

But right now, their faces aren't so happy go lucky. They're definitely not chipper. Or maybe it's the goggles and the hardhats. Maybe their expressions are being masked. But then, I don't need to see their faces clearly to know they're scared. Hell, I am too. What we're about to do is not only illegal, it's downright spooky. We're about to mess around with the dead. The body we're about to dig up is hardly even cold yet. His ghost could still be wandering the earth. This cemetery is full of ghosts, and it's a frightening place even during daylight hours.

Naturally, I think of the old man. What would he do?

He'd swallow his fear and enter the unknown, full speed ahead, damn the freakin' torpedoes.

"You guys ready?" I call out.

"As I'll ever be," Baily says, both his gloved hands gripping the side bar on the canopy frame.

"I was born ready, Baker man," Twigs assures.

He's holding on to an identical side bar on the opposite side of the canopy with one hand while he reaches into the cab with his other. He turns the hand into the claw, brings it within inches of my face, but stops just short of touching it.

"Let's do this already," he says. "I'm getting hungry again."

I shove the gear shift into first.

"Hang on, fellas," I announce, "this is gonna be one hell of an adventure."

I take the cemetery road slow, but not too slow. I have the Times Union photo of the Menands grave in my pocket just for reference, but I know where I'm going. Pops and I have walked just about every square inch of this place studying the graves of civil war vets and other graves of now long dead famous statesmen, writers, painters, architects, and diplomats. All ghosts that haunt the place at night.

The darkness would be all-consuming if not for the moon, but it's still pretty thick nonetheless. The stark light that shines from our round headlamps onto the branches of the old oaks make them look like crooked arms on giant monsters. An animal scatters across the road. My heart flies up into my throat. I hit the brakes, and my two amigos nearly fly off the machine.

"What the hell, Baker?" Baily barks. "You trying to get us killed?"

"Sorry," I swallow. "A fox just crossed the road. Scared the crap out of me."

"At least it wasn't a black cat," Twigs points out. "Maybe foxes are good luck. Right?"

"Yeah," I say. "Unless it's a werewolf."

"Now, why do you gotta go say something like that?" Twigs barks his high-pitched tone as if reaching for an even higher note.

Suddenly, something swoops out of the air.

"Hell was that?" Baily asks.

"Jesus, it's bats," Twigs points out. "There's loads of them. This place is a freakin' scary movie. Freakin' Halloween."

A flock of bats take flight from out of a tree further down the road. We can see them reflected in the headlights. Tiny black, leather-winged bats flapping rapidly, making sharp turns and arcs in the night sky. I feel them buzzing by the backhoe cockpit, which means those two guys must feel them whizzing past their heads.

"I don't like this place," Twigs says. "It feels like we entered into another dimension. You know, like Twilight Zone reruns. Like we've walked through the looking glass into an ancient haunted forest." He clears his throat. "Three best friends in search of an ancient cross said to possess mystical powers," he goes on in his best imitation of Rod Serling, "suddenly find themselves not inside a cemetery, but in the Twilight Zone."

"Keep joking, Twigs," Baily says. "But seriously, Baker, let's roll already. Before somebody comes."

I toe-tap the gas, pull forward.

We pass acres of heavily wooded graveyards on both sides of the road. Some of the graves are simple, represented only by a single humble headstone. Others are ornate and huge—marble mausoleums that could double as small churches or stately homes. One such mausoleum is owned by a family named Frankfurter. Another by Schafer, as in Schafer Beer. Some of the headstones are relatively new and in good condition. Others are old, graying, and covered in weeds. These are the graves of the long forgotten, Pops claims. These are the ghosts that are said to have been wandering the cemetery the longest.

The further I drive into the heart of the cemetery, the more I feel a cold sensation running up and down my backbone. It's almost like we're driving into a lake, only the water is having no effect on our lungs. We're not getting wet, but the air is noticeably cooler, thicker, heavier. At least, that's the way it feels to me.

The headlights pick up a shadow, a silhouette that shoots across the road.

Once again, I tap the brakes, come to a stop.

"You see that?" I ask, heart pumping, brain buzzing with adrenalin.

"See what, douche bag?" Baily says, his voice showing signs of stress.

"Yeah," Twigs says. "I didn't see nothing."

Maybe they're lying, or maybe they're telling the truth. Maybe my eyes are playing tricks on me. But I swear to God above, what I just saw cross the road was a human figure, and since there's no one else crazy enough to be in this ancient haunted cemetery at night, it can only be one thing. A ghost.

Or maybe I'm just scared. Scared out of my wits. Crazy scared.

Maybe I'm seeing things—scary shit I'm making up in my imagination. Maybe it's time I got my crap together and handled this situation like a man—like a professional sandhogger. The way Pops would want me to handle it.

"There's no such thing as ghosts, right?" I whisper to myself.

"What?" Twigs begs. "You say something, Baker man?"

"I'm gonna blacken your other eye you don't get going," Baily says.

There's an ancient cross that needs liberating. And I'm gonna be the one to do it. Me and my two amigos. Chase the afraid, but also, Chase the confident.

I drive another few hundred feet until I come to the landmark I've been looking for. The monument of Albany Mayor, Erastus Corning.

"This is it," I say out the open canopy window. "Corning's future grave."

It stands tall and imposing in real life. Like an ancient obelisk we've just managed to uncover in the middle of a jungle. A Celtic cross-topped obelisk.

"So then, where's Menands?" Twigs asks.

Wishing I'd brought along a pair of binoculars, I scan one-hundred-eighty degrees. But then, knowing that a pair of night vision binoculars aren't exactly the kind of thing Pops keeps in his tool arsenal, I don't wish for too long. I grab the flashlight stored on the cockpit floor and shine it in the direction I believe the Menands grave to be. That's when I see it. The big green awning that appeared in the Times Union newspaper picture. The grounds crew hasn't removed it yet.

"Amigos," I say. "That's it. We found it."

I look at Baily. He's smiling. I turn, glance at Twigs. He too is smiling, nodding slowly, confidently. Confidence is a hell of a lot better than being anxious.

"Well, all right, Baker," he says. "Let's freakin' go digging."

VINCENT ZANDRI

I spin the backhoe wheel to the left and motor up

the slight incline toward the Menands grave and the

Cross of the Last Crusade.

CHAPTER 9

Positioning the backhoe at the foot, of the Menands grave, I engage the hydraulic stabilization legs which raise the big back wheels off the ground. I spin my seat around and man the backhoe controls.

Baily and Twigs flank the long grave. Twigs with a shovel in hand and Baily with the flashlight, the light of which is now shining on fresh dirt.

"Sure you know what you're doing, Baker?" Baily questions.

"Hey," I say, "I was born working a backhoe."

Truth is, I've never worked the backhoe without the old man positioned right behind me, just in case I should pull the wrong lever and what's supposed to go up goes down or what's supposed to go right goes left, and vice versa. But the old man isn't around to watch my back on this one. This time, I'm on my own, and I'd better get it right. Chase the determined, or is it Chase the downright stupid?

In my head, I hear Pops' words. *Tickle the controls, don't pull them. Let the machine do the work it was designed to do. Don't force anything. If you get into trouble by pulling the wrong lever, just let it go, and it will correct itself. But most of all, don't swing the boomstick too fast when you have a full bucket, or you'll tip the tractor over entirely. A full bucket is half a cubic yard and weighs at least twelve hundred pounds. I've seen more than my fair share*

of men killed or injured for life doing exactly that,
Son.

That in mind, I swallow something dry and bitter
tasting. I place my hand on the controls and pull
down on the first lever. The stick rises. The boom
groans. With its sharp three-inch teeth, it looks like
an old dinosaur suddenly come back to life. The
tractor engine revs, and the hydraulic hoses fill and
go taut. I feel metal clashing against metal, and the
vibrations travel throughout my flesh and bones. I
push the control forward, and the bucket drops.
Push it forward a little more, and the tractor lifts
while the bucket bites into the ground. I tickle the
center control, and the bucket scoops up its first full
mouthful of fresh dirt. I'm so excited, I pull back
hard on the third control. The bucket makes a full

ninety-degree swing so fast and so abruptly, the machine tips up on the right-hand stabilizer.

It's exactly what Pops warned me about.

Out the corner of my eye, I see Baily go flat on his back while he narrowly avoids being crushed by the flying bucket. I feel myself going over, and all I can think about is how I'm destined to die at only fifteen-years-old and inside a haunted cemetery no less. At the same time, I'm also thinking this: I've screwed this treasure hunt up even before it's gotten started.

But then something wonderful happens. The backhoe tractor doesn't tip over. It falls back onto the left stabilizer, the big metal machine banging and swaying and groaning, but otherwise intact.

"What . . . the hell . . . was that?" Baily gripes, as he slowly raises himself from off the ground, wiping the dirt from the back of his overalls. "You ain't never forgiven me for that black eye, and now you're trying to get me killed. Is that it?"

"Yeah, Baker man," Twigs chimes in. "I thought you were an expert sandhogger. Just like your old man."

I feel the warmth of embarrassment wash over me like a waterfall.

"Ummm, my bad fellas," I say from up in the cockpit. "Let's just say I got a little over-excited."

"Let's just say you're a douche," Baily retorts, his face angry and redder than a Chinese lantern.

Tickling the control, I dump the load of dirt and then carefully reposition the bucket back over the grave. I dig in once more and take out a second load of dirt, dump that. It only takes three more bucket scoops until we make out the sound of metal against concrete.

I stand.

"Baily," I command, "flashlight."

He aims the bright light inside the hole. Twigs, shovel in hand, jumps down into the hole. He turns to me.

"You got some chains, Baker man?" Twigs asks.

"We got 'em," I say.

"Good," he says. "Because once we get this concrete lid removed, the only thing that separates us from that old crusader cross is a little bit of wood and metal."

He smiles because we're close. Even Baily smiles.

I climb down from the cockpit, grab the chains off the side of the backhoe, hand them down to Twigs.

"You know what you're doing?" I ask.

"Hey," he says, "I'm a mechanical genius."

He snakes the chain under the two metal handles then attaches it to the metal bucket.

"Give her a lift, Baker man," Twigs orders.

I climb into the cockpit, and gently as she goes, push back on the control. The bucket raises, the chain goes taut, and the lid begins to lift off the burial vault. Twigs proudly rides on top of it like a swashbuckling movie hero. Baily takes hold of the lid to keep it from swinging wildly, and I gently set it down on the grass beside the pile of dirt. Aside from the dirt, it will be the last thing to be set back into the grave when the time comes to clean this mess up.

"Okay, Baker brother," Twigs says, detaching the chain from the lid. "Let's check out this Menands dude."

He jumps back down into the hole, and I reposition the backhoe and the chain over the casket. Twigs attaches the chains to the casket's long side handles and, with his long tall body bathed in the flashlight's white light, he once more rides triumphantly atop the casket out of the hole and onto the damp ground.

I jump down from the cockpit and take my place by the casket. Heart pounding in my chest, I can hardly wait to see the cross for real.

"Crap," Baily says, kneeling over the casket, his gloved fingers touching an ornate locking device. "It's locked. You need a key."

"What the hell do they lock it for if he's dead?" Twigs poses.

"So idiots like us can't rob him blind," I point out. Then, "I've got an idea."

Hopping back up behind the backhoe controls, I raise the bucket.

"Stand back gentlemen," I warn. "This is going to take all of my sandhogging powers and skill."

"Who the hell's he think he is?" Baily says, his eyes on Twigs. "Doug Henning, the magician?"

Pushing the bucket control forward ever so gently, I set its teeth directly on the casket's lock. That's when I push the control forward a touch more, and the lock snaps off just like if it was made of balsa wood and not metal. I pull the control toward me. The bucket, stick, and boom retract accordion style back into an upright position.

"Good work, Baker," Baily offers. "You are sort of a magician with that thing, once you get going."

Twigs slowly reaches out with his claw, grabs Baily's face.

"It's magic!" he bellows.

"You're a screw ball, Twigs," Baily scolds, his goggle covered eyes peeled on the now unlocked casket. Then, turning to me. "Who wants to be the first to open that thing up?"

I can't help but laugh as I jump down from the cockpit onto the ground.

"Don't tell me you're scared, Baily," I say before turning to Twigs.

"Twigs," I go on, "put that claw to good use and open it up."

He takes a quick step back.

"You're the real treasure hunter," Twigs claims. "You do it."

I swallow something that tastes like gravel. They're right. I'm the one who's always mouthing off about hunting down some of the world's most prized relics and treasures and then writing about them in my pulp novels and comic books. That is, when I learn how to write someday. But it's true. I'm always bragging about the adventures I've already shared with the old man in all those exotic Middle East, Asian, and Banana Republic destinations. And I'm always talking about getting my two amigos to join me. Two plus one equals three amigos. Right now, they're looking at me to be their guide. Their captain. It's time for me to step up and face the great unknown . . . head on. Chase the fearless leader. Well, you can scratch the fearless part. Because right now, as I grip the casket handlebar with both hands, I feel like I might just crap myself.

"Get ready with that flashlight, Baily," I demand.

He shines the light on the black coffin lid.

"Here we go," I announce. "Lifting . . ."

I pull the lid up and expose the insides of the casket.

And that's when Twigs passes out.

VINCENT ZANDRI

CHAPTER 10

"**B**reathe, Twigs," I say, waving my hard-hat over his face like a fan, sending cool air onto his pale face.

His eyes suddenly open. Open wide.

"What the hell happened?" Twigs asks, voice strained.

Baily is just about pissing himself he's laughing so hard. "You passed out, idiot," he says through a hail of snorts and laughter.

"It's okay, Twigs brother," I say. "Happens to the best of us. I recall getting lightheaded when the old man pulled the lid off one of those basket mummy caskets we dug up in the mountains of Peru. Or come to think of it, maybe it was the altitude sickness."

Grabbing an arm a piece, we help Twigs back up to his feet.

"What about the cross?" Twigs questions. "Is it there?"

Baily aims the light for the casket interior.

"Well, yabba dabba freakin' doo," he says. "What we got, ladies and germs, is a whole lot of nothin'."

I take a step forward, grab the flashlight out of Baily's hand, shine it up and down the casket interior.

"You're not kidding," I say. "There's nothing here."

"No cross, no body, no nothin'," Twigs says. "It's empty like my stomach. Just a whole lot of stale air."

That's when we notice a rustling in the bushes on the other side of the road.

"What was that?" Baily almost whispers.

More rustling.

We turn.

I shine the circle of light onto the trees and brush. Someone is running from out of the bushes and down the road. Someone or something ghost-like.

"Hey, you!" I shout. "Stop!"

The person stops, about-faces. With the light shining on his face, I'm able to make out exactly who our intruder is. And it's not a he. It's a she.

"What the hell are you doing here?" I shout.

CHAPTER 11

She's wearing black jeans and a black hooded sweatshirt, her long hair pulled into a bun. With the hood on, she looks like a tall, slim boy. But with the hood off, she looks like the most beautiful girl ever—Monique. But that doesn't mean I'm not pissed off at her for sneaking up on us like that. And if I'm pissed off, I'm sure the other two are about ready to dump her into Menands's empty grave.

"I just wanted to help," she says, her arms nervously dangling by her side.

"Help," I say. "How did you even know we were here? This is supposed to be a secret mission."

Her face goes tight. She crosses her arms over her chest.

"And very illegal, in case you didn't notice, young Mr. Baker," she adds.

"Chase, what the frig is going on?" Baily shouts at me from the thick darkness across the road. He's still not sure about the identity of our visitor.

"Listen, Monique," I say, placing my hand gently on her hip. "You've got to go back home. This is no place for a girl."

What's the saying? If looks could kill? Well, thank God they can't because the look she gives me would pretty much destroy me if that were the truth. She brushes my hands off her hip.

"What the hell does being a girl have to do with anything?" she grouses.

Okay, I don't know a whole hell of a lot about girls, but I can tell you this. If I don't back step my comment just a little, there will be hell to pay for the rest of the school year. Hell hath no fury like a high school girlfriend who's mad at you. Because, if she's mad at you, then all her girlfriends are mad at you too. You face days and days of walking the hallways to sneers, jeers, and snide whispers from an all-female army.

"I'm sorry, Monique," I declare, bowing my head just a little. Girls are suckers for contrition. Or so Pops tells me. "It came out all wrong. What I meant was, I *really, really* like you. And there's some danger involved in what we're doing, and I don't want to see you get hurt. That's all."

She purses her lips, re-crosses her arms, and exhales.

"I still think you and your friends don't want me around," she says. "But I guess I can forgive you." Her attitude goes from pissed off to curious in three seconds flat. "So, what are you doing? Robbing a grave?"

"Not exactly," I say. "We heard Pierre Menands was buried with a very ancient and historic cross made of solid gold. A cross that was said to be carried by the Knights Templar during the very last Crusade in Jerusalem back in the twelve or thirteen hundreds. I think it's wrong to bury something that significant for the rest of eternity, so we're digging it up for the sole purpose of delivering it to a museum."

"And collecting quite the reward for it, no doubt," she says slyly, her arms still crossed over her luscious chest.

"And maybe that," I say, not without a grin.

But here's the thing: Monique doesn't look to me like she's about to turn tail and head back home just because I ask her too. Looks like she's staying whether I like it or not, or whether my amigos like it or not. Best to make the best of the situation.

"Chase!" Twigs yells. "Maybe we should rebury this thing before it gets too late."

"Coming!" I shout over my shoulder. Then, to Monique. "So, whaddaya say? You wanna become an official treasure hunter?"

"Why not?" she says, uncrossing her arms. "But it sure feels like grave robbing to me."

That's when I make out the sirens.

CHAPTER 12

The sirens are getting louder by the second. Then comes the flashing red and blue lights. Bright headlights and rooftop flashers lighting up the entry to the wooded cemetery.

"Oh shit," I say, my mouth going dry and my pulse pounding in my throat. "Run, Monique. Run like hell."

I take her hand, and together we sprint in the direction of the Menands grave.

"Cops, amigos!" I shout. "Cops coming our way!"

Baily is standing by the backhoe, foursquare.

"What the hell is she doing here?!" he shouts. "Did she bring the cops with her?"

"Watch your mouth, Baily!" Monique bites back. "You know damn well the only reason you're mean to me is because you're in love with my ass."

Baily's face goes stone stiff and red as a blood blister. Clearly, his tongue is tied in knots because that quick wit of his has been placed on pause like a cassette deck. He's been bitch slapped, and we all know it. Twigs starts to laugh, but then presses his claw over his own mouth.

"Laugh it up, beanpole," a clearly embarrassed Baily mutters after a time.

But it's time we can't afford.

"Just let's get the hell out of here," I insist. "I'll have to come back for the backhoe."

"You don't gotta tell me twice, brother Chase," Twigs says, tossing his helmet and goggles into the open grave. "Where too?"

I look over one shoulder, then the other.

"We can't go in the direction we came, because the cops will be on us in a flash."

The sirens grow louder. More bright lights flash through the darkness. I peel off my goggles and hardhat, toss them into the grave along with Twigs' stuff. Baily does the same. Hopefully, Pops won't notice they've gone missing or it will all come out of my allowance.

"Downhill," I say. "We're gonna bushwhack downhill, and we're gonna lose them."

"And then what?" Baily questions.

"We're gonna go after that cross," I say. "And I think I know just where to find it."

"Where, Chase?" Monique asks.

"The Pierre Menands mansion."

We run.

Across the road and over the plots, trying our best to avoid crashing into the countless headstones and monuments that seem to be hidden under cover of darkness. Baily nails one head-on, falls to the ground.

"Jesus H. Christmas," he moans, his voice strained and in pain. "Can't we use the freakin' flashlight already?"

Sirens. Lots of them . . . getting louder. Closer.

"They're following us, Baily," I answer. "They must have split up, some of the cops figuring we'd head downhill. We use the flashlight, we'll give away our position."

Baily gets up. I can barely make him out in the darkness with the tall trees and clouds concealing the little bit of moonlight coming from . . . what's Pops call it? The waxing moon.

"I'm okay, thanks," Baily mumbles sarcastically under his breath. "Nothing broken, fellas. Don't you worry about me."

More sirens. Then, bright headlights and flashers breaking through the darkness on the narrow road that leads to the downhill section of the cemetery.

"No time to talk," I insist. "Run."

We run downhill as fast as we can, the distant cop cruiser headlights giving us just enough light to see in between the stones and mortuaries. My heart thrashing in my chest. My breathing grows shallow, pulse pounding in my temples. Monique is keeping up with me on my right-hand side while my amigos are on my left. By the time we come to the bottom of the hill, no more headstones grace the flat landscape. There's only a dirt road that runs north/south and beside it, the train tracks. Behind us the sirens are getting louder and louder, the lights breaking through the trees. Looking over my shoulder, I see more sets of headlights and bright, colorful flashes. More cop cars coming from the south.

"Cripes," I say. "They're coming at us from every direction."

"We're surrounded," Baily points out. "I'm too young to go to jail."

"No giving up," Twigs says. "Chase will figure something out. Won't you, Chase?"

All eyes are on me as the cop cars bear down on us like hungry vultures about to tear into raw meat.

Chase the Johnny-on-the-spot.

I look left. Nothing but open road. The cops will easily catch us if we go that way. We can't exactly go back uphill either. If we cross over the train tracks, keep moving toward the east, we'll drown in the Hudson River since its banks are less than a half-mile away. We can't go right because the APD is bearing down on us from that direction.

Then, out the corner of my eye, I catch sight of something.

The train tracks lead to a trestle bridge that spans a narrow length of river inlet. On the opposite side of the bridge is the small village of Menands which is cut off from the cemetery and the all the roads leading into and out of it. If we can get over the bridge, we just might have a shot at avoiding the cops altogether and gaining access to old man Menands' mansion and the Cross of the Last Crusade. No guarantees, but what other choice do we have?

I feel myself growing a smile.

"Boys and girl," I say. "Follow me."

"He's smiling, Twigs," Baily says. "Douche is smiling. And I don't like it when he smiles 'cause usually something on my body gets banged up. I don't like pain. It hurts me."

"Very astute, Baily," Twigs agrees. "Usually when Brother Chase starts smiling over a plan he's cooking up in that big round head of his, it means he's reaching for some mortal danger, and yes . . . lots of pain to go with it."

"Don't talk about it," I command, grabbing Monique's hand, leading her directly for the train tracks. "Just do it."

"Hey," Twigs says. "That might make a cool commercial one day. Just do it."

We run, the sirens getting louder and louder as more and more cruisers descend upon the bottom of the cemetery's hill. When we reach the tracks, I don't let go of Monique. Instead, I head in the direction of the metal trestle bridge.

"Chase," Monique screams, trying to pull herself free. "Are you crazy? What if a train comes?"

I turn to her while running.

"There are no trains this time of night," I insist. It's a lie. I have no idea if trains do or don't run at night. But, I work up an even bigger smile. "Trust me."

When we come to the bridge, I stop.

Because it's a bridge, there's no packed gravel railroad bed to support the length of tracks. If we want to cross it, we'll have to be careful to step onto each individual wood railroad tie. If for any reason, our feet slip off the ties or miss the ties altogether, it's a drop of one hundred feet or more to the raging white water river inlet below.

Monique looks at me like I'm crazy for even considering this plan. So do Baily and Twigs. The sirens wail louder. The cop cars are now heading in our direction.

"Listen, guys," I say, "we have no choice. It's either this or be arrested for grave robbing. And you know what that means? It means juvenile detention and a grounding by your parents that will last until your thirty." I raise my hands, exhale. "Listen, anyone who doesn't want to chance the bridge, I won't hold it against you. I understand. Fear can be a real bitch. But sometimes, just sometimes, facing that fear head on, balls out, can be one hell of a stimulant."

"Jesus H. Christ on a stick, you're crazy, Baker, you know that?" Baily spits. "When we get to the other side, I'm gonna give you that second black eye. And I'm gonna enjoy it."

"That's the spirit, Baily," I encourage him. "Twigs brother?"

He swallows something that looks like a brick inside his long neck.

"If I don't make it," he says, holding out his claw of a hand. "Tell my mother I was *reachinngggg* for something special in my life. The chance to do something pretty cool. Pretty great. Return the

Cross of the Last Crusade back to its heavenly home in Paris, France. I betcha my old man is watching me right now, bitches."

"Monique?" I beg.

"Will you hold my hand?" she asks, sheepishly.

"It will be my pleasure," I say. "Just follow my lead, and we'll all be fine."

Inhaling a deep breath, I release it slowly.

I step onto the first of the bridge's railroad ties, then extend my leg over the empty, seemingly bottomless space so that I safely plant my foot on the second railroad tie. It's the first of many steps over troubled waters while I silently pray that this isn't the hugest, most dumbass, most moronic mistake of my young life.

The space between each tie is about eighteen inches, give or take. In other words, about half the length of your average stride. But that's okay, because all it means is that I'm taking twice as many steps to cover the same distance as if I were walking on solid ground. It takes only a minute or so to make it a third of the way across and even less to get halfway once I have a rhythm going.

"How you doing, Monique?" I ask over the roar of the river. Thick, misty spray shoots up out of the gorge from the angry white rapids below.

"Just don't let go!" she insists.

I feel her hand in mine. It's cold and damp, wet from the slick watery mist. I'm gripping her hand so tight, I'm afraid I might break her bones. I continue with my pace until it happens. The mist covered wood ties are slicker than I thought and my sneakered covered foot slips off a tie.

I go down onto my right knee while my left shin jams against a solid wood tie. The pain is so intense and electric, I feel like I'm about to pass out. I see stars dance around my head in the darkness. I pray nothing is broken.

Monique screams. I'm yanking on her hand. For a quick second or two, I feel like she's about to step into the space between the ties and make the plunge into the river. That happens, she's as good as dead. I'm as good as dead too since I'd be making the trip south along with her.

Ignoring the pain, I raise myself up, regain my balance. Mist is rising from the river, coating my face and hands. The roar of the water against the rocks below echoes in my ears. Gazing over my shoulder, I steal a glance at Monique. Her face is pale with fright, but otherwise, she's okay. I peer over her shoulder, get a look at Baily and Twigs. They're slowly but surely making progress. But I can see that with his long, gangly legs, Twigs is having trouble maintaining his balance. Jesus H, he has trouble keeping his balance on flat land. Between the mist, the slippery ties, and making the trek in the dark, it's all going far slower than I thought it would.

Maybe this was a bad, moronic idea after all.

But then, what the hell difference does it make at this stage of the game? No choice now but to keep going. Turning back toward the opposite side of the bridge, I take another step. Monique follows, her hand never letting go of mine. Not even for a second. It's like we're not holding hands. More like we're biologically attached.

Another step, the roar of the inlet is so loud it's drowning out any hint of cruiser sirens. I feel like I've entered a whole different world from the one that exists outside of this bridge and the gorge it spans. Another step . . . and another. I can make out solid ground on the other side of the bridge now. It means we're making progress, getting closer. The mist is no longer ascending into our faces. It's behind us now. The worst part is behind us.

Confidence fills my veins, makes me feel all warm and fuzzy inside. Like it's suddenly Christmas Eve.

We're gonna make it, Chase man . . . We're gonna outsmart the cops and get our hands on that ancient cross after all . . .

The sudden sound of a train whistle cuts through the noise of the roaring gorge. It also frightens the living snot out of me, right down to my very core.

CHAPTER 13

Night becomes day.

It's like God flipped a switch and turned on the lights. I turn quick. I'm blinded by the bright headlamps on the speeding freight train bearing down on us. The rails tremble. The ties bounce up and down. The old metal trestle bridge creaks, shivers, and hums under the sudden strain of the oncoming multi-ton engine.

Monique screams something not from her lungs, but from somewhere deep down within her soul. A primal scream accompanied by fear so real you could poke a hole through it. I pull her to me before she passes out, falls to her death.

"Holy fuck!" Baily screams. "We're gonna die!"

He starts sprinting over the ties until he trips, goes down flat on his belly. For a split second, I'm convinced he's about to slip through an open space and drop into the roaring gorge. But he miraculously bounces back to his feet on one of the ties. He keeps moving, never mind the slick boards.

Twigs is another story.

Twigs does the wrong thing. He stops, turns, stares at the oncoming train like a deer caught in the headlamps of an oncoming pickup truck. I try to shout, but my voice won't come. I clear my throat, work up some moisture in my mouth.

"Twigs!" I scream, "Run! Run for your life!"

It takes a second or two. But the conductor, who must see us by now, lays on the horn. It's so loud it seems to shake Twigs out of his state. He turns and, like Baily before him, begins leaping across the ties.

"I don't wanna die!" he screams. "I don't wanna die! I don't wanna die!"

"Monique!" I shout. "We've got to go as fast as we can!"

But she's not moving. She's stone stiff. Petrified. I don't think about what I have to do. I just do it. Bending at the knees, I wrap my arms around her legs and throw her over my shoulder. From that point on, I don't carefully walk the railroad ties. I leap over them. There's so much fear and adrenalin injected in my veins, Monique's weight doesn't even register.

The train whistle is deafening.

Brakes screech and squeal. The tracks rattle and vibrate so violently I feel it in my bones and teeth. The mist is blinding me. I can't see or hear them, but I know Twigs and Baily have got to be screaming. Screaming for their lives.

Then, when I finally reach the end of the bridge, I toss myself and Monique off to the side, roll down an embankment, my head slamming against a rock, and . . .

I'm riding a horse.

YOUNG CHASE BAKER AND THE CROSS OF THE LAST CRUSADE

It feels strange because I've never before been atop a horse, much less know how to maneuver one. Not with my short legs. I'm surrounded by men dressed in armor. Big, stocky men, with white capes draped over their metal bodies. Branded on the capes are bright red crosses. We're armed with swords, daggers, quarter-staffs, crossbows, and longbows. When I look down at my hands, they're covered in blood.

The day is bright and hot.

The mid-day sun beams down on the vine and tree covered hills to my right-hand side and the massive gray-white stone walls and minarets to my left. It comes to me then, this is the place where Jesus Christ lived and prayed. This is also the place he was put to death. It's been taken over by Muslims, and we've come on behalf of the Pope to take it back. To take it back in the name of Rome and the Holy Spirit.

A man lies on the ground. He seems to be a man of great importance. His helmet has been removed revealing a pale face bathed in agony. The more I focus on him, the more I am drawn to the gash in his chest. It runs diagonally, from his left shoulder all the way to his right kidney. Dark red blood pools all around him. How he isn't dead already, I'll never know.

The circle of men splits to make way for another man. This man isn't wearing armor. He is, instead, wearing a long brown robe. His hair is cut like someone put a bowl over it and trimmed around the edges. The center of his skull has been shaved bald, creating a ring of hair rather than a full head of hair. He's a holy priest, and he is holding a cross— one made of gold with precious stones embedded into it. The cross radiates brilliantly from the sun shining down upon it. Or maybe it shines for another reason altogether. Maybe it's blessed by the good Lord himself.

We all wait silently with bated breath. Even the horses are still as the priest bends over the slain crusader. The breeze blows steadily. It howls and whistles through the crooked branches of nearby olive trees. In the distance, singing, chanting voices of a thousand Muslims who still control the eastern side of the city echoes. The priest raises the cross as if presenting it to God. He chants a prayer in Latin, the same words over and over again. I've never taken a single Latin lesson in my life, yet somehow,

I know precisely what he is chanting.

O dear Jesus, protect us from the lies which offend God.

Protect us from Satan and his army.

Help us to love You more.

Sustain us in our battle.

Defend us in our faith.

Lead us to Your refuge of safety.

Help us stand up and defend Your Holy Will.

Quite suddenly, a radiant beam of sunlight—

brighter than all the others—shoots out of the sky

and hits the cross. The gold cross seems to fill with

so much energy that it trembles in the priest's hand.

He has no choice but to grab hold of it with both

hands.

When the beam of light suddenly disappears, the priest slowly sets the cross on top of the slain crusader's chest. He's praying the same words louder now, more rapidly, more forcefully, as the cross is vibrating and humming.

"Sustain us in battle, Templar Knights!" he shouts. "Slay Satan! Defend our faith!"

Something more miraculous happens then. The chest wound begins to close. The bleeding stops. The pool of blood disappears as if somehow having seeped back into the crusader's veins. Life returns to his face. The painful expression that once filled it becomes an expression of peace, tranquility, and happiness.

The crusader sits up, makes the sign of the cross from his forehead and over his chest. We all follow suit, making the sign of the cross, reciting the words in Latin.

"In the name of the father and the son and the holy spirit."

The priest removes the cross and bows before the crusader who now stands, sword drawn, pointing it at the heavens.

"With this cross," he shouts, "we are one with God! We cannot be defeated!"

We draw our swords and release a collective roar that shakes the stone walls of Jerusalem . . .

When I come to, I shake my head and realize that only a few seconds have passed. But my crazy dream—a vivid dream like I learned about recently in physical science class—seems like it lasted for at least ten minutes. I peer up at the bridge. I see Twigs running like hell, his gangly legs thrusting out before him in rhythm, his long arms swinging, his mouth and eyes wide open. The train's headlamp bathes him in white light, and its whistle drowns out his shrieks. There can't be ten feet separating Twigs from the train's nose when he comes to the edge of the trestle bridge and jumps off the rail bed, dropping into the gulley opposite the one Monique and I are in.

The train conductor releases the brakes and the train speeds past, its many freight cars rattling and trembling on the metal tracks. I turn, search for Monique. She's seated on her backside, her knees pulled up against her chest. Her black hair is almost invisible in the darkness. But after a few seconds, the clouds open up for what seems the first time that night, to reveal a brilliant full moon. Now, her smooth, silky hair reflects the rich light. Seconds ago, we were nearly run down by a speeding locomotive and somehow all I can think about is wrapping my arms around her.

It's exactly what I do.

I take her in my arms. She leans into me, shifts herself so that her face is only inches from my face. Her sweet rose petal scent wafts in the air. I can feel her heart beating against mine. Or maybe what I'm feeling is the pounding of my own heart. Only this kind of pounding has nothing to do with fear any longer. It's all about melting into the arms of the one girl I've loved since kindergarten.

I press my lips against hers. My entire body lights up as if an electrical charge has been inserted into my soul. Our lips and tongues play with one another. For a split second or two, I feel like I might actually pass out.

"Are you freakin' kidding me!?"

Releasing Monique, I turn quick, peer up at the top of the railroad bed embankment. It's Baily, standing four-square, his hands clenched into fists.

"I was just about to check on you guys," I say, wiping my mouth with the back of my hand.

"How hard were you trying?" Baily barks.

Then, another figure appears in the moonlit night. Tall and lanky, his knees still trembling. Twigs.

"Remind me why I love you again, Brother Baker?" he asks, his already high-pitched voice an octave higher than normal.

I burst out laughing. Grabbing Monique by the hand, I pull her up the embankment with me and greet my amigos. I slap Baily on the shoulder.

"We made it, didn't we?" I say. "We beat that train, but most of all, we beat the cops."

I'm laughing and feeling pretty damn good about myself, even if I did get a solid knock on the noggin. Bringing the tips of my fingers to my skull, I trace them over the tender bruise that's risen under all that hair.

"What next, smarty pants, Baker?" Baily begs. "Only a matter of time until the fuzz come looking for us again."

I turn toward the old neighborhood situated between the Pierre Menands Memorial Little League ballfield and the big white Montgomery Ward building. A neighborhood that's a throwback to the old Victorian days of the 1890s, the houses—or mansions—are as big as our high school. The biggest mansion of all is owned by Menands.

"Here's the deal, fellas," I go on. "We started out believing Menands was dead. That he was buried in the Albany Rural Cemetery just this morning. Thanks to Baily's mom, rumor had it, that buried along with him was a cross of mega-historical significance and value."

"Primo screamo value," Twigs adds.

"Exactly," I agree. "Primo screamo value. But here's the thing."

"Menands ain't dead," Baily interjects.

"We don't know that for certain, Dylan," Monique adds, finger-combing her long hair in a way that makes me want to dive into it.

"There's was a whole lot of air in that coffin, missy," Baily snips.

I hold up my hands.

"Okay, okay," I say. "Everyone get along. We're all in this together. And we still have a mission to accomplish that yes, might be illegal in the eyes of the law, but perfectly legal in the eyes of God. You might even call our quest to return the cross to its rightful owners the *last* true crusade."

"Jeeze, you hear yourself?" Baily questions.

"He's *reachinggggggg* for brilliance," Twigs says, waving his claw in the air.

In my head, the memory of the vivid dream I had when I was passed out plays. The cross being used as a tool for healing a man who appeared to be mortally wounded. I can only wonder if the cross isn't speaking to me.

"Maybe this sounds crazy, guys," I say, "but what if the cross truly is blessed by God?"

Baily's stone-cold face grows a hint of a grin.

"How hard did you hit your head again?" he begs.

"I'm serious," I say. "What if the cross possesses some kind of spiritual power and that's the reason Menands wasn't in the grave at all?"

"Still not following," Monique adds.

"You're scaring me, Baker," Twigs barks. He raises his stick-like hands, shakes them around. "Scarrrrrring me."

I hold my hands up once more like I'm saying, *hold your horses*.

"Okay, okay," I press. "Look, at the very least there was a reason Menands wasn't buried in his coffin this morning, and I can bet it has to do with that cross."

"So, where is the damn cross if it's not in the damn ground along with its damn owner?" Baily asks the ten-thousand-dollar question.

"It's here," I say.

"Where's here?" Twigs asks. "And will there be food?"

"Here," I repeat, "inside the forgotten-in-time

village of Menands. Mr. Pierre Menands' mansion,

to be precise."

VINCENT ZANDRI

CHAPTER 14

The plan, as I relay it to the other three, is this: we approach the old mansion from the back. Sneak in through the kitchen window, just like Twigs and Baily did my place this afternoon. All we have to do is cross over the ballpark, try not to catch the attention of any cops that might be patrolling the neighborhood, head around the back of the mansion, sneak in, grab the cross, and we're home free.

"You make it sound easy peasy," Baily says.

"It ain't never that easy," Twigs adds.

"We have to trust, Chase," Monique says, squeezing my hand. "He knows what he's doing. Don't you, Chase?"

She leans in, gives me a peck on the lips.

"Jeeze. I'm gonna puke," Baily says.

"Hand me the lariat," Twigs begs. "I wanna hang myself."

I ignore them. "Follow me," I command. "Radio silence the whole way. No flashlight."

We continue along the rail bed for another hundred feet or so until we come to the short chain link fence that surrounds the ballfield.

"Climb over," I order.

Each of us easily climbs over the fence into the outfield. The grass has recently been cut, and the sweet damp aroma fills our nostrils. The air is cooling down now that it's after eleven o'clock and any cloud cover that existed when we first started this hunt has all but disappeared. Above us is a clear sky full of stars and a brilliant full moon.

We cross the infield and slink past a dugout only to find the gate to enter the field is locked. We quietly scale the gate without incident. What lies before us now is a village road that runs perpendicular to the fence. It's lined with old oak trees that must be at least as old as the Victorian homes lining both sides of the street. On our immediate left is a not a house but a stone church. It's made of dark fieldstone, and it contains a bell tower on its back end. It reminds me of something you'd see in an old village in the French countryside.

Beyond the church is the first of a dozen houses constructed in a bygone era. Two and three-story wood clapboard homes with massive wraparound porches, dormers, stained glass windows, ornate moldings, and tall, arched slate roofs. Majestic houses that must have cost a fortune to build back in the day. The carpentry alone must have taken some wicked skill.

We move along the road as stealthily as possible. We don't want to attract the attention of anyone who might still be awake in the sleepy little village. On our right is the local library, a small white bungalow with a tall brick fireplace sprawling up one side of the front porch. It must have been somebody's house at one time. Beyond it is a wooded lot, and beyond that sits a small stone bridge that spans a narrow creek bed.

YOUNG CHASE BAKER AND THE CROSS OF THE LAST CRUSADE

When we cross the bridge, we come to the Menands
property. It's far more massive than any of the other
properties we've passed. As if those were owned by
Menands' support staff back when he was the head
honcho at Montgomery Ward—the man who sat
way up in the high white castle. The front lawn
alone nearly takes up one full acre and the white
four-story colonial home that sits atop a second and
third acre is big enough to fit four or five versions
of the house I live in with the old man.

The place is dark this late at night. But the moon is
furnishing enough light that I'm able to lead
everyone to the edge of a thick strip of woods that
lines the northern perimeter of the property. Not
that I'd ever met him in person, but I'd always
known of Menands as a cranky old dude, so it won't
surprise me one bit if he has security cameras set up

in all sorts of secret places. Closed circuit television set-ups are becoming all the rage now that cable TV is available for just about every household in the country.

It's pretty amazing when you think about it. Televisions that no longer require an antenna. Televisions that offer up to twenty-four stations, plus a brand-new movie channel called Home Box Office, or HBO for short. Pretty soon, you won't even have to leave your house to go to the movies. What's next, personal home computers or even portable phones that don't require wires? Whatever it is, I'm sure dudes like Menands will have it first.

We gather at the edge of the woods.

"Okay, everybody," I whisper. "Stay close. We walk along the edge of the woods until we reach the back of the house. Then, we scoot along the back lawn, blend in with the shadows to avoid the cameras. By then, we'll find a good place to break in without making a huge racket."

The others nod.

"Let's hope this goes better than the bridge crossing," Baily says.

"I'm still shaking," Twigs says. "But then, I'm starving too."

"You got a tapeworm, Twigs," Baily interjects.

"I trust you, Chase," Monique says. "Whatever you suggest is fine by me."

"Oh, for the love of God. I'm gonna toss my cookies a second time," Baily adds, working up a hawker and spitting it.

"Gross, Dylan," Monique says. "Keep it up with the jealousy, and I might just have to marry Chase Baker one day."

My heart melts. This time, it's me who kisses Monique on the cheek.

Then, I add, "Who else wants a kiss?"

"That's gay," Baily says. "I ain't no homo."

"Maybe later," Twigs says, puckering his lips.

I start walking.

We walk the extensive tree-line, covering more than the length of a football field before we reach the opposite side of the big house. I offer up a hand signal to indicate it's time to cross over the lawn to the backside of the house. I go first—my body crouched, taking it double-time over the trimmed flat lawn. Monique follows. Then, coming up on her tail, Baily. Finally, Twigs.

I scan the house's back lawn. There's a built-in swimming pool surrounded by a stone deck and a short chain link fence. A large rectangular patio is filled with outdoor furniture. Expensive stuff painted white. There's even a small putting green beside the swimming pool, and beyond that, a tennis court. Menands sure liked his country club sports.

I examine the house. A set of immense wood and glass doors give access to the house from the patio. My guess is the doors are locked and dead-bolted. But just to be sure, I whisper for everyone to stay put while I try them out. I make my way to the doors, grip the opener on the closest leaf. I attempt to turn it.

Just as I thought.

Locked.

I try the second door.

Locked.

I take another step back, examine the entire back of the house. The windows are closed, meaning we're not going to get in by busting through a screen. For a second or two, I feel my optimism fade. I had originally thought we'd break in through the kitchen window, but I'm not sure it's possible. We've come all this way only to find that Menands' mansion is impenetrable. The other three are looking at me, counting on me for direction. Monique with her hopeful face. Baily with his cynical glare. Twigs with his happy-go-lucky-I'm-hungry grin.

I see it then. Out the corner of my eye. At first, it doesn't register with my brain as looking like much of anything. Just a square panel inlaid in the bottom of the second leaf off the back patio. But the more I focus on it, the better I can tell that it's a door within a door. You know, one of those cute little doors for cats and dogs. It gives me an idea.

"Twigs," I say in a forced whisper. "Come here."

He jogs over to me.

"What's up?" he asks, eyes bright, his too fast metabolism in full swing. "We goin' in through the kitchen window?"

"Locked up tighter than a jailhouse," I say.

"So, how we gettin' in, Baker man?"

"Through that," I say, pointing directly at the doggy door panel.

He shakes his head.

"Umm, Baker. You mean like through that little door? You want us *all* to go in through that teensy-weensy door? It's not even a door, it's a panel."

"Yes," I say. "That's a little door inside the door meant for the dogs and cats. You, my special amigo, are the only one of us who can fit through it."

"You're kidding me, right?" Twigs poses.

"No," I say, patting his shoulder. "You crawl in through the little door, then unlock and open the big door for us."

"What if there's an alarm?"

"We'll cross that bridge when we come to it."

Twigs just looks at me for a minute like he's looking not at one of his best life-long friends, but instead at craziness personified. He raises his hand, makes the claw.

"My brother, Chase Baker," he says. "Always reachinnnnnnng . . . Always pushing the bubble."

I shush him. There's no telling how far his high-pitched voice will travel. The others gather around us.

Baily asks me the plan. I tell him. He laughs. "This I gotta see," he says.

Monique voices her concern about an alarm system. I tell her about the metaphorical bridge and how we'll cross it when we come to it like I did Twigs.

We've been learning about metaphors in English this year, and it makes me feel smart.

"You always say that about everything," she says. "Crossing the bridge, I mean."

"So does my pops, it turns out," I say. Then, turning to Twigs. "Let's get this show on the road, pal."

Twigs inhales and exhales. "You can count on me, Brother Chase."

I tell him we'll hold back out of sight until he's in. That way, if something goes wrong, we can all just head for the woods.

"Oh great," Twigs says. "Meanwhile, my ass will be grass."

"We truly understand the sacrifice you're making for the team, Twigs," I go on. "Just like the

Vietnam vets the old man hires for his excavating crews. Some of them are narrow and skinny like you. They were the brave badasses who volunteered to go down into those rat holes in the jungles of Nam. They were the real heroes, Twigs. The real men. Just like you, man."

His face is now full of pride. "Okay," Twigs announces. "I can do this."

He scoots off on his way to the back doors off the patio. When he comes to the little door within the door, he drops down to his knees and pushes the panel open. Like a gopher entering its hole, he presses his arms flat against his side and sticks his head into the opening. From there, his torso disappears and finally his legs and feet.

He's in.

Monique grabs my hand. "I hope he's okay," she says. "If something happens to him, I'll never forgive myself for allowing you to talk him into this thing."

"You mean, you won't forgive *me*," I correct her.

"You're right, it's you I wouldn't forgive," she agrees.

Suddenly, the sound of a lock being unlatched breaks through the quiet, then a squeak of hinges and a door opening. It's Twigs, and he's waving us on.

"Let's go," I say.

Together, we jog across the patio and enter the door.

Twigs closes it behind us. "Now what?" he asks.

"Let me get my bearings," I say, taking a look around the dark room.

As far as I can tell, it's what Pops would call a sitting room. Leather chairs and couches spread throughout the giant space. The walls are covered in bookshelves. There's also an enormous desk set up at the far end of the room. Menands' old desk maybe.

It gets me to thinking.

"We might be closer than we think to the cross," I say. "Stay right here."

I make my way over to the desk. Pulling out the flashlight from my pant waist, I thumb the light on. Then, inhaling a half breath, I pull the top drawer open.

VINCENT ZANDRI

And then the alarm sounds.

CHAPTER 15

If only it were just the alarm we have to worry about. But along with the blaring horns and flashing emergency lighting, comes the barking of not one dog, but two. Cripes, maybe three.

"Exit!" I shout. "Now."

The three about-face. Baily grabs the door handle, tries to open it. But it won't budge. A great rumbling occurs from above. The entire house trembles like there's an earthquake.

"Baily!" I shout. "Get the hell away from the door!"

That's when iron bars drop from the ceiling, covering not only the doors and windows but the entirety of the interior walls. It's like a prison magically appearing around us.

Baily turns, the redness of his face visible even in the darkness between the flashes of security lighting.

"We're locked in!" he shouts as his Adam's apple bobs up and down in his neck. "No escape. No exit. What the hell did you get us into, Baker?"

The dogs continue to bark and growl. But I don't see them.

Chest grows tight. Heart pounds.

"Now, just take it easy, Baily," I insist. "We can just send Twigs back through that opening."

"And how am I supposed to slip through the bars?"
Twigs asks. "I'm not *that* skinny. Maybe the cops
are on their way."

He's got a point. Make that two points. Chase the
dazed and confused.

I feel it in my gut. The self-reliant gut Pops has
been trying to help me develop since I was six years
old. Hell, since I was born. This isn't about the cops
coming to arrest us or, for that matter, to rescue us.
This is about three helpless flies being caught in a
trap we created for ourselves.

"Chase," Monique says, her meek voice barely
audible over the buzzing, pulsating alarm. "I don't
like this at all. I feel like we're about to die."

The alarm stops but the lights continue to flash. An
eerie quiet settles in. I feel like the slate floor is

about to open beneath me. Footsteps break the silence.

A man appears from what I take to be the kitchen, his dark silhouette almost mammoth against the bright flashing lights. He's holding two chain leashes, each one attached to a large German Shepherd. The dogs are no longer barking, but they are growling, bearing white fangs that glow in the flashing white emergency lighting.

"You are closer to the truth than you know," bellows the big man, his voice baritone deep, his accent most definitely not American, more like something European. East Germany, maybe. Romania. I've never been to Romania, but I've seen enough Dracula flicks to know what I'm talking about.

"We got a big problem," I say, swallowing hard.

Monique issues a noise that sounds part shriek and part I'm-about-to-faint.

"Do something," Baily says.

"I wanna leave now," Twigs adds.

The alarm lights shut off, descending us into total darkness. A hissing sound begins from somewhere under our feet, a sweet mist or vapor. I inhale a breath. My head spins, my knees buckle, and then nothing.

VINCENT ZANDRI

CHAPTER 16

A beam of new moonlight that struck the Crusader's cross now disappears. The explosion it makes as the light is once more swallowed by the darkness is powerful enough to unsettle our horses, and in some cases, make them rear. Flames from our torches shine light on the now miraculously healed man. Slowly, he gets back up onto his feet. Although he is no longer bleeding, dark red blood stains his armor and his cloak.

He raises his sword to the heavens.

"I am Sir Henry!" he shouts, his voice thunderous and booming. "And I will have my revenge upon Saladin!"

When I come to, I try to move my arms, but I can't. It takes a minute or two for my vision to return. When it does, I can't believe what I'm seeing. We're all chained to a stone wall by our ankles and wrists. There's no natural or electric light, but instead, burning torches mounted to the wall by metal holders.

A stone altar sets in the center of the room. Though room isn't the right word for this place. More like a dungeon. A dungeon I can only assume is located directly under the Menands' mansion. A body is laid out on the altar entirely covered with a white sheet. It might not be much of a wild guess, but I can only assume the body is that of Pierre Menands.

Footsteps—heavy and laden—descend a set of stone stairs to my right. A man appears, his massive body taking up the entirety of the opening in the wall, the top of his big round head nearly touching the stone arch above the opening. I know this man. But then, something tells me there's no way I've ever met him before. At least, not in this life. That's when it comes to me.

He is the man from my dream.

He's the man healed by the crusader cross one thousand years ago in Jerusalem. But how the hell can that be? It's crazy to believe that a dream can mimic real life. A dream is made up of a bunch of crazy subconscious thoughts all tossed together into a brain blender. But the two dreams I've had since this little adventure began tonight were both vivid and pretty damn real. Not like dreams at all. More like memories. It's as if I was there all those years ago in Jerusalem. It's like I've known this man for centuries and now our lives have somehow crossed paths again. And what's the common denominator in all of this?

The Cross of the Last Crusade.

Is it possible the cross is speaking to me? Channeling its message directly to my brain?

"Sir Henry," I say, pronouncing the name in the traditional French like, *Enryyy*. "You are Sir Henry."

"Who the hell's Sir freakin' Henry?" Baily presses.

In all my shock and confusion, I didn't even think to check on the well-being of my friends. I peer over one shoulder, then the other. Baily is looking at me with an expression that tells me he's gonna kill me if he ever gets out of those chains. Twigs is still out cold. In fact, he's snoring. Then I glance over to Monique who is most definitely wide awake and trembling with fear. I'm so close to her I can see tears streaming down her face.

She looks at me.

"Chase," she says, "what in God's name is going on here?"

In my head, the memory of the crusader cross receiving a beam of light from the new moon, its powers healing the man who'd been slain on the battlefield. That man was Henry. He was healed almost one thousand years ago, and yet here he is as alive, massive, and powerful as he was the day he held his sword up to the heavens in defiance. The day he cursed God for allowing Saladin to slay his men and himself.

I recall a story my old man told me during a dig he took me to in Jerusalem. The evil Saladin, leader of the Muslim hordes who sacked the city and took the temple mount for their own, murdered thousands of Christians. Christians who were crucified, burnt at the stake, drawn and quartered, or beheaded. Among those killed during the crusades that followed were Sir Richard and Sir Henry of Paris. But legend had it that both were healed of their mortal wounds when touched by The Cross of the Last Crusade when the light of a new moon passed through its gemstones. Sir Richard eventually died but not until many decades later. However, Sir Henry's death date was never recorded. Maybe because he never really died.

"What we're about to witness, Baily," I say, "is a resurrection."

Sir Henry steps further into the room. A long brown robe with a hood covers his head and shields his face—like something a holy man might wear. Strapped around his waist, however, is a leather belt to which a broadsword is holstered. He goes to the body, pulls away the white sheet exposing Menands' naked corpse.

"I'm going to be sick," Monique says.

"Don't look at it," I insist. "Keep your eyes closed."

"I'm dreaming right?" Twigs says, his voice gruff and course as he slowly regains full consciousness. He rattles his chains, pulls on them like it's possible to break out. "I'm in a nightmare, and all I have to do is go back to sleep and wake up under my Superman blanket."

"It's all too real," Baily informs him. "Save your strength."

Sir Henry reaches into his cloak, pulls out a cross. *The* cross. Even in the semi-dim fire-lit room, the gold along with the inlaid gems, is a brilliant sight to behold. He lifts the cross up to the heavens.

"With this cross of powerful Abaddon," he exclaims, in French-accented English, "I will raise up our brother, Pierre, so that he might live for all eternity."

A light appears from a narrow opening in the upper portion of the stone wall to our right. It's almost like whoever designed this basement dungeon knew precisely where to place the opening in order to catch the light of the new moon on a certain night, at a certain time, which I'm assuming to be midnight.

Moonlight beams through the opening, catches the gems on the cross. The cross lights up as if a power switch has been triggered inside it. It even begins to take on an audible hum, like it's alive.

"What's that?" Baily forced out. "Why's the cross acting like that?"

"It's power," I say, my mouth going dry with both fascination and fear. "It's the power of God."

"Now I *know* I'm having a nightmare," Twigs says. "They never told us when we were altar boys that God was actually real."

"I can't help it," Monique admits. "I have to look, Chase."

I pull my eyes away from the cross just long enough to see that she's stopped crying. Her curiosity has taken over.

The cross begins to shake in Sir Henry's hand like his human strength isn't a match for its supernatural power. That's when he lays it flat onto Pierre Menands' chest.

The light beam turns into a glow—so bright it lights up the entire basement.

Abaddon.

I know the word. It means "destruction" in Hebrew. It can also mean the devil. If you don't believe me, ask the old man. He's the one who educated me in all this hocus pocus in the first place ("You'll never learn this from a school book, Son," he once told me on a flight to the Middle East, his thick notebook open on his lap, its many pages chock-full of detailed notes and sketches. Like something DaVinci would have kept on his person 24/7).

I'm confused as I watch. How can a symbol of God be used for evil purposes? It's almost like the cross has undergone a kind of spiritual kidnapping. Like that movie Pops still won't let me watch on HBO, The Exorcist. I know humans can be possessed, but can relics be possessed too?

"I'm scared, Chase," Monique cries.

"I told you not to look at it."

"I can't help it," she replies.

Then it happens. Something entirely out of this world. Menands' body begins to convulse—his chest heaving, his arms and legs shaking like the limbs on a tree caught in stormy wind gusts. His mouth opens, and his tongue protrudes from his mouth like a pink snake.

"You gettin' all this, Baker?" Baily barks. "'Cause I might be seeing it, but I ain't believing it."

"That tongue," Twigs cries out. "It's reaccchhhinnngggggg . . ."

Good old Twigs. I almost burst out in laughter. But then, what the hell am I thinking? Now's not the time for jokes. We're chained to some freako creepo sadomasochist's basement wall. A basement he went out of his way to have constructed like a medieval dungeon, complete with torches, a ritual table made of stone, and chains bolted into the walls for prisoners. We're watching a priceless ancient artifact being used as a means for putting life back inside a very stone-cold dead body. My guess is that after the main event is over, Sir fucking Henry is gonna make Swiss cheese of our bodies with that long sword of his.

Oh well, it's been a short life, but a crazy good life . . . I mean, what the hell, I haven't even gotten laid yet. Not that I would admit that to the amigos.

Chase the damned.

I refocus on the cross. The light emanating from it is so bright it hurts my eyes to look at it. The noise is deafening and only getting louder. I shift my eyes back to Menands' face. It seems to be regaining color. Going from chalk pale to pink like the blood is flowing back into it. Could it be really happening? Am I witnessing a resurrection? Like the kind that happened to Jesus Christ himself?

Or maybe what's happening is something else altogether.

What if the scene I'm witnessing is an exorcism of some kind? What if an evil spirit is slipping inside Menands' body and taking it over? Yeah, sure, I watch a lot of sci-fi movies. Who doesn't? I've seen that new movie, Halloween, on HBO and the other new one, Poltergeist at the drive-ins. Scared the living crap out of me, both of them. But what I'm watching right here, right now, makes those flicks look like Grandpa's home movies.

Menands' head moves.

It turns slowly on its thin, wiry neck until finally, it faces me. Faces us.

When the eyes open wide, I feel like I might pass out.

Monique screams. So does Twigs. So loud I hear them over the noise from the cross. I swear my eardrums are about to burst. I steal a quick second to look at Baily. His eyes are shut. His face is beet red from the stress. From the fear. And I get it. I'm so afraid I feel like my heart might explode. But something else inside me is keeping me going. Something that prevents me from shutting my eyes, as if I could just pull a blanket over my head and make the evil disappear.

It's curiosity. Like looking at the bloody aftermath of a brutal car wreck. You don't want to look, but you can't help yourself. It's either in your blood, or it's not. As for me—Chase Baker, treasure hunter— curiosity no matter how morbid, is most definitely swimming around in my bloodstream. I got it from Pops. I am half him, so it only makes sense. But what's the old saying? Curiosity killed the cat?

I stare into the old man's eyes. They stare back at me. Mesmerize me.

Menands lifts his arms, makes fists with his hands.

How the hell can this be happening?

"He's reachinggg," Twigs shouts.

"Reachhhhhhinggg, and he's supposed to be dead. Wake up, Twigs. Wake up, Twigs, already!" His voice holds no hint of amusement.

The show doesn't end there. Menands raises himself up as though his spine were made of a heavy-duty spring instead of bone, muscle, and tendon. Sir Henry draws his longsword, bows down reverently on one knee.

"You are now one of us, Pierre Menands," he states. "You have beaten death, much like I have beaten Saladin."

"Salad who?" Baily says.

"I'll explain later," I tell him. "Or maybe you should pay more attention in world history class."

The beam of new moonlight ceases suddenly.

The glow from the cross disappears along with the loud, electric rattle and hum. Pierre Menands lifts the cross from his lap and kisses it. He then holds it over Sir Henry's hood-covered head.

"May we live forever more, Sir Henry," he says, his voice not that of a man who died of old age, but of a far younger man. A man younger than Pops anyway. But from what I know, Menands died in his nineties. How can he be young again? Only way I can think of, is that he made a pact with Abaddon. The destruction. The devil. I guess what it all means is this: when he kisses the cross he's not kissing God. He's kissing God's enemy. Menands goes on, "Now, it is time we give to the power what the power deserves."

Sir Henry places the cross back inside his leather satchel. He then turns to the three of us and extends the business end of his long-sword in our direction and issues an evil smile.

"And now," he says, his voice deep, brutal, and frightening, "you will feed the power."

VINCENT ZANDRI

CHAPTER 17

"What's that mean?" Twigs begs. "We're gonna feed the power. What's this guy, like a serial killer food connoisseur?"

"I think it means he wants to cut us up like pork chops," Baily says.

"I think I wanna go home now, Chase," Monique says. "Date officially over."

Sir Henry removes his hood with his free hand. He approaches us, holding the sword out straight like it's a lance. Meanwhile, Menands slides off the table, wraps the sheet around him to cover himself up. He's no longer an old man at all, but a well-built man maybe in his twenties or thirties. I'd seen pictures of him taken recently. Pictures in the newspaper. He was a fragile old man with a crimped spine and a bald scalp mapped in brown age spots. He couldn't even walk. He was forced to use an electric wheelchair to get around.

Now, he's young. The cross has reversed the aging process entirely. I guess you could say, the cross possesses the same powers as the fountain of youth.

It's a miracle, right?

But something's not right with this version of ol' Mr. Menands. It's his eyes. While I hang there, chained to the wall, I can't help but look into eyes that aren't brown, or blue, or gray-blue for that matter. They're just white. And inside the white is a

circular black spot. He's staring at me and grinning.
The grin is not a pleasant grin, but instead, a kind of
nasty, I-can't-wait-to-see-you-impaled-with-Sir-
Henry's-sword kind of grin. Not that I've ever seen
one of those before.

Sir Henry comes closer and closer. And stops.

"So, who wishes to have the pleasure of being the
first to be sacrificed to the great Abaddon?" he
bellows.

"He does," Baily says. "The short, stocky guy on
my left. This was all his idea. My mom works for
Mr. Menands. I'm like family to him. Aren't I, Mr.
Menands?"

"Thanks a lot, Baily," I reprimand. "With friends
like you—"

My thought fades because something else steals my attention—the sound of barking. Loud barks resonating against the stone walls that make up the staircase leading down into this suburban hell hole. Sir Henry's German Shepherds appear bearing their fangs, clear mucous dripping from their mouths. It's like they haven't been fed in ages. But now, they know they're about to feast on flesh. Human flesh. Our flesh.

"Chase," Monique says, "just when you thought things couldn't get worse."

"Nice doggy," Twigs offers, his voice so tight and stressed I can barely hear it. "Nice . . . doggy."

The dogs come forward, growling, muscular shoulders hunched, heads lowered, like they're about to pounce even before Sir Henry stabs us with that old sword. Meanwhile, the new and improved Pierre Menands keeps staring at us, not saying a word, not making a move, not even blinking. Like his new eyes no longer require moisture.

"Do something, Baker," Baily demands, struggling to free himself of the chains that bind him. "Do something, or I promise I'll find a way to kick the crap out of you in heaven."

"That is, we make it to heaven, Baily," I say. "But mark my word, old friend, you'll have every chance to beat me up down here on earth before the night is out."

"Don't make promises you can't keep, Baker," Baily adds.

"Everybody get along," Twigs insists. "We're altar boys for God's sake. We should exit this life like altar boys."

"I wasn't an altar boy," Monique says.

"One day," Twigs adds, "they'll let girls be altar boys. They might even let girls be Boy Scouts too. You wait and see. Errr, you know what I mean."

"Silence!" Sir Henry commands.

An electric shock runs through my system. It's the same thing that happens when my homeroom teacher screams for us to shut up. Like Sir Henry, Mr. Berner has a loud, booming voice. He's also a boozer, which means he's usually hungover and nasty in the mornings. If there's one benefit to dying young, it will be never having to see his ugly face again. But then, what the hell am I saying? Chase the suddenly pessimistic.

Sir Henry takes another step forward then shifts a few steps to the left. He raises the sword, points it directly at Twigs' long turkey neck, poking the flesh.

"So," Sir Henry says. "Who shall be first? Shall it be you, skinny young man?"

Peering over my shoulder, I focus on the indent the blade is making in Twigs' neck. All it would take is one single thrust of the blade, and one of my best amigos would be Hamburger Helper. But Sir Henry retracts the blade, takes a couple of steps to the right. Once more raising the blade, he pokes Baily's neck.

"Or how about you, tough young man?" Sir Henry poses.

"What *about* me?" Baily retorts, strong, defiant. I have no doubt he'd take a swing or two at the big Sir Henry if he could only free his hands. Baily's a trained boxer. Maybe he'd even accomplish what Saladin couldn't one thousand years ago. Maybe he'd knock the big bully onto his ass the way Rocky punched out Apollo Creed. Or should I say, the way Rocky and Apollo punched each other out.

"I see you consider yourself quite the adversary," Sir Henry says. "Perhaps you would have made a formidable crusader. You would have slain many Muslims in God's name."

"Maybe I'll slay you instead," Baily sneers.

"Don't push him, man," I say. "This guy is looney tunes."

For a split second, I'm convinced Baily's had it. That he's pissed off Sir Henry enough that the old crusader is going to run his blade right through my amigo's neck. But something comes over Sir Henry. He works up a smile. Like he enjoys Baily's spunk and tough guy persona. Call it bravery or call it stupidity, but for now, Baily's defiance is saving his life.

Sir Henry moves to his right two more steps. He puts the blade against Monique's neck.

That's when I lose it.

"Leave her alone, you son of a bitch!" I scream. "She's just a girl! What kind of animal are you?!"

The entire dungeon goes still. Sir Henry's smug expression fades. Menands' grin disappears. Even the two German Shepherds stop growling. It's like no one has ever challenged their authority before. As though I'm the first man, or teenager anyway, to ever yell into Sir Henry's face. Baily was tough and defiant, but I'm being downright belligerent. And to be honest, it feels damn good.

Sir Henry pulls the blade from Monique's neck. He shifts himself a few more feet toward me until his face is within inches of my own. So close, I can smell his foul breath. He positions the tip of the sword up under my chin. He presses the point so hard against the soft flesh he breaks the skin. The sting shoots up into my skull, sends anicy shock down my spine. For a split second, I feel like I might faint.

Sir Henry turns to Menands.

"Monsieur Menands," he says, "we have found our first sacrifice."

Menands nods. "You may proceed," he says in this deep, zombie-like voice. "The dogs, they are getting very hungry."

VINCENT ZANDRI

CHAPTER 18

My heart jumps into my throat. Stomach drops to somewhere around my ankles. The dogs resume their growling and barking along with lunging at my ankles with their fangs. Not quite digging in but getting nibbles all the same. Taunting me. Torturing me. What the hell kind of mess did you get everyone into now, Chase Baker?

Sir Henry verbally orders the dogs to heal. He then holsters his sword and reaches up to the shackles that bind my wrists. He releases them. I drop to the floor . . . hard.

"Hey, let him go!" Baily yells.

"Leave him alone!" Monique screams. "He's just a kid like us!"

"Come on, man," Twigs says. "He's was only kidding around with you. He didn't mean nothing. Let him go, Sir Henry dude. Let *us* go. We won't tell a soul about the setup you've got down here. You can have all the fun you want playing knights of the crusades or vampire knights or Monty Python and the Holy Grail or whatever the hell you're into. Just let us go."

"The time for that is past," Sir Henry says while unshackling my ankles.

The wind has been knocked out of me. My head is spinning. I think I might have broken my nose and possibly a tooth. Pops is gonna kill me if I broke a tooth—if I survive. Sir Henry uses his superhuman strength to drag me across the stone floor by the neck of my shirt. He yanks me up onto my feet. Then, wrapping his arms around my waist, he hefts me up onto the table.

"Lie back," he demands.

"What if I don't want to?" I say.

He turns his attention to the dogs and barks an order out in French. The dogs immediately lunge for Monique's legs.

"Okay, all right, stop!" I shout.

He issues another order, and the dogs stop just short of tearing into my girlfriend's shins. I'm able to catch a quick glance at her face. Her eyes are rolling around in their sockets, and her face has gone sickly pale. She's about to faint. In all honesty, I hope she does.

Stealing one last glance at Twigs and Baily, they both lock eyes with mine. The expressions on my amigo's faces are not like, *see ya later, Baker*. It's more like, *rest in peace*. I swallow something bitter and dry, lie back onto the hard, cold stone table. That's when Sir Henry immediately goes to work tying my wrists and ankles to all four ends of the table. Reaching into his robe, he pulls out a half-moon shaped dagger.

Then, shifting his focus to Menands, he utters, "At your command, Monsieur."

Menands' zombie face lights up like this is the most fun anyone can have with their clothes on. Or a bed sheet toga.

"You may proceed, Sir Henry," he says, voice guttural and awful. He follows with a loud, ear piercing laugh that's sharper than the knife in the old crusader's hand.

My heart is pounding so loud, it sounds like a Peter Criss kick drum thumping inside my brain. I'm seeing the world through a haze of red, my pulse soaring, my mouth having lost all moisture. How the hell I managed to get us into this mess, I'll never know.

Wait a minute. Scratch that.

I know how I did it.

I did it not by being overly curious, but by being selfish. By thinking I could do something important like returning the cross that was to be buried forever to a museum where the entire world could enjoy it for centuries to come. How could I pass that kind of opportunity up when Baily first revealed they were going to bury the cross along with Menands' body?

"He's gonna take it all with him," Baily's mother had told him.

But that's when it hits me. *He's gonna take it all with him.* Isn't that what all the adults say when a rich dude dies? A rich dude who was known to have been stingy? Maybe the cross was never going to be buried with Menands after all. Oh, well, doesn't matter now, does it?

Gripping of the knife handle with both hands, Sir Henry raises it high, prepares to plunge it hard and deep into my chest.

I close my eyes tight.

"Here it comes," I whisper to myself. "I'm coming, Mom."

A loud, short, sharp burst fills the room along with a brilliant flash. The knife falls from Sir Henry's hand, and whether by the grace of God or just plain good luck, falls into the space between his body and the stone altar. For a split second, his eyes lock with mine before they roll into the back of his skull. A dark red stain expands over the area where his heart is, and he collapses.

The basement fills with police. Police dressed in protective tactical gear just like they used to do on a Sunday night episode of S.W.A.T. back when I was in junior high. The now very much alive Pierre Menands runs around the table like he believes he's gonna escape.

"Down on the floor, Myers!" the head policeman shouts while shouldering an automatic rifle. "Get down! Hands up!"

A dozen red dots appear on Myers's head and chest.

Myers? Who the hell is Myers?

He drops to his knees, raises his hands.

"Don't shoot," he cries. "I'm unarmed."

Three policemen quickly surround him, push him to the floor face-first, cuff his wrists behind his back while another crew releases my friends from their chains.

"Easy!" Myers shouts as the cops pick him up, start dragging him out of the basement. "I got my freakin' rights, you know."

His accent is most definitely not French. More like Brooklyn, New York. Or maybe Queens. Pops would know. Speaking of Pops, he suddenly comes barreling down the stairs.

"Chase!" he barks. "You all right, kid? Jesus, you had me worried."

I sit up, slowly.

"I am now, Pops," I say.

He wraps his thick arms around me, gives me a big chested bear hug. Then, releasing me, he takes a step back, looks me up and down as though making sure I don't have any physical wounds. He's dressed in his dirty khakis, denim work shirt, the pockets filled with slips, old work boots, and an old leather coat. He's also wearing a ratty old green baseball hat that says CAT, like the tractor.

He clears his throat.

"Now that I know you're okay," he says, crossing his arms over his chest, "you're gonna have some serious explaining to do. But first, we'll get you and your friends home to their parents. Poor folks must be worried sick."

I glance at my two amigos. Three when you count Monique. All of them are looking at the floor like they're too afraid to look my old man in the eyes.

"You kids came awful close to getting in some serious crap," Pops says after a time. "You know that, don't you? Digging up a coffin is a state offense that can land you in juvenile detention for a half dozen years."

Baily takes a step forward. "True, Mr. Baker," he says. "But Menands was supposed to be buried with

The Cross of the Last Crusade. It's worth a ton of dough."

"The cross," I whisper, sliding off the altar, reaching into Sir Henry's robe, careful not to stain my fingers with his blood. I take hold of the cross and pull it out.

It's heavy in my hand. Heavier than I originally expected. Like a gold brick with precious gems inlaid in it. Maybe this mission, however dangerous or stupid, just might be totally worth it.

"Holy cow," the old man says, "I'll take that."

He holds out his hand. Begrudgingly, I hand it to him.

"It belongs in a museum, Pops," I announce. "You taught me that. It needs to be studied. It's got special powers. We've seen the powers. Right guys?"

They all nod.

"Well, I'll see that it gets to the proper authorities," Pops says. "I imagine it's state's evidence right now." Then, motioning toward the stairwell. "Come on, let's get going."

"Wait," I said. "Who's Myers and where's Menands?"

The old man turns around. He says, "According to the police, that guy Myers . . . he was in cahoots with Menands' life-long Butler."

"But when we dug up Menands' grave, there was nothing in it."

"That's because Menands' real body was shipped back to Paris where he wished to be buried with his family. He didn't want to insult the people of his village namesake, so they put on a mock burial. Happens all the time. He really cared about the people who lived here and the people he employed."

He's gonna take it all with him . . . Wrong. Menands wasn't selfish at all. Deceptive maybe. But not selfish.

"But why the sicko ceremony?" Baily asks.

"Yeah," Monique says, "they wanted to kill us."

"And feed us to those nasty, rabid dogs," Twigs adds.

Pops shakes his head. "My best guess is you guys entered a situation that was beyond your control. That butler—"

"—Sir Henry," I say.

"What?" Pops asks.

"Sir Henry," I repeat. "He was killed by Saladin one thousand years ago, during the last crusade against the Muslim hordes in Jerusalem. But the magic powers of the cross brought him back to life."

The old man gazes at the dead man lying on the floor. "It ain't working so well now, Chase, is it?"

"Ain't that the truth," I say.

"His real name is Leo Dibello," Pops goes on. "He is, or was, a real sadomasochist. I'm wondering if

Menands even knew about this sicko basement set up down here."

The lead cop comes back into the room. He's tall but built like Stallone.

"We need to take care of that body folks," he says. "I don't have to tell you kids that your parents are going to be notified, and you're all going to have to come in tomorrow to give statements. Right now, the cemetery isn't pressing charges for what you did, but that doesn't mean the DA won't." Glancing at Pops. "Mr. Baker, technically speaking, the kids stole your tractor and other equipment. You can press charges if you wish."

Pops turns to me, eyeballs me while addressing the cop.

"Pressing charges would be letting my son off *easy*," he says, a sly grin forming on his ruddy face. "Now, let's go, kids."

We head up the stone steps, make our way outside to Pop's Jeep. I take the shotgun seat while the three amigos squeeze into the back seat. Pops starts her up, pulls out of the driveway.

"My mother's gonna kill me," Baily moans as we head onto the main road.

"Mine too," Monique mumbles. Then, "Ummm, Chase, I don't think we should see one another for a while, except at school, of course. I don't think my dad will allow it."

Easy come, easy go, I think. But I can't blame her or her dad.

The inside of the Jeep goes quiet for a time until Pops passes by a Wendy's, then a McDonalds.

"Say, Mr. Baker," Twigs says, his high-pitched voice sort of guarded. "You, uhhh, you wouldn't happen to be a little hungry, would ya?"

Pops cracks a smile.

"Jeeze, Twigs, it's almost one o'clock in the morning," Pops points out. "You nearly lost your young life tonight, and all you can think about is chowing down?"

"Danger makes me hungry," he says.

"Everything makes you hungry," I say.

"Tapeworm," Baily adds. "It's gotta be a freakin' tapeworm."

That's when Pops does something that shocks even me. He slows the Jeep to a crawl, spins the wheel hard, makes a U-turn. He drives until he pulls into the only all-night burger joint in town.

"Okay," he says, "you might as well grab something to eat now. It's gonna be a long night for all of you. My treat."

"Gee, thanks, Mr. Baker," Baily says.

"Yes, thank you, Mr. Baker," Monique echoes. "That's sweet of you."

"Thanks a bunch, Mr. Baker," Twigs says as a claw-like hand quickly comes reaching around, wrapping around my face, pulling it toward the passenger window. "And don't forget, you never know when the *clawwwww* is coming for you!"

THE END

If you enjoyed this Young Chase Baker action/adventure, you're going to love the first novel in the Chase Baker Thriller series, The Shroud Key. Here's a sample of the award-winning action thriller:

THE SHROUD KEY

```
(A Chase Baker Novel #1)
```

VINCENT ZANDRI

PROLOGUE

Florence, Italy

October 2012

"You stole my wife!"

That rather inflammatory accusation is lobbed from a fully-grown man who, despite his God-given gender, is most definitely screaming like a girl. A high school math teacher, to be precise, who's attempted two back-to-back roundhouse swipes at me and whiffed miserably.

"I did not steal your wife," I insist in as calm and unthreatening a voice as I can possibly muster under the circumstances. "Your wife stole me. Get it?"

Here's the deal:

I'm standing outside the Duomo Cathedral in

beautiful, scenic Florence, Italy. No, that's not right. I'm not standing. More like I'm dancing, dodging the punches and swipes of this paunchy, Dunkin Donut fed middle-aged American. The American wants me dead. Dead and buried. Yet I feel terrible for him. His chubby face has gone heart-attack red, eyes swollen with tears and rage. His horrified wife looks on as do a crowd of tourists who have come to the Duomo to witness some glorious Renaissance history but instead have managed to acquire free ringside seats to a brawl between a walking tour guide and one very jealous husband.

How did I get here? How did guiding these nice mid-western white-bread Americans result in my pulling the rope-a-dope inside one of the most sacred piazzas in the world while in the distance the polizia alarms blare, and the crowds of Japanese gawkers look on in smiley faced astonishment?

The sad truth of the matter is this:

I did it by being me. Chase Baker, former sandhog turned bestselling thriller writer, slash private investigator, slash tour guide, slash full-time screw up when it comes to some of the more attractive female clientele.

So what harm can come from a little innocent flirting?

Just ask the man desperately taking swings at me, trying to knock my teeth down my throat.

Maybe this isn't the first time easy love has come my way via a tour client, and this isn't the first time a jealous husband has wanted to hurt me over it. It's just that this is the first time things have gotten physical in public, with potential clients looking on. So then, like a freshly dug grave that's caving in on all sides, I suddenly find myself way in over my head.

But then, this rather sensitive situation is not entirely my fault. For example, it's not my fault that the woman in question rang my doorbell at midnight last night, waking me from out of a sound sleep just to "chat" and drink a little Chianti together. Not my fault that I'm still the same not-entirely-worse-for-wear Renaissance man I was the day my now ex-wife walked out on me holding my infant daughter in her arms, shouting, "You don't want a marriage! All you want is a plane ticket to anywhere but here!"

What is my fault, is my having answered the door for this exceptionally attractive tourist in the first place. Better that I simply rolled over and ignored the ringing doorbell. Better that I shut out the image of her lush blonde hair, jade green eyes and legs so long and firm they began at her feet and ended somewhere inside her shoulders. Better that I reminded myself of her marriage status and then simply dozed cozily back to sleep.

But, of course, what made things worse is that the lovely tourist woke the dog. And once Lulu, your two-year-old black and white pit bull is awake, half the residents on the Via Guelfa are awake from her barking and carrying on.

Dragging myself out of bed, I ran my hands over my short hair and down my scruffy face. I stretched myself one way and then the other, feeling the solid muscles in my back and arms tense up. Opening the shutters onto the cool spring night, I felt the cool air touch my naked skin, and I laid eyes upon the blonde apparition thumbing my buzzer.

"It's midnight, Mrs. Doyle," I said out the open window. "I'm closed for business."

In the background, I could make out the noise of some revelers returning from the bars near the Piazza Del Duomo, their boot heels slapping against the cobble-covered roads.

"I just want to chat," she said, smiling, her alcohol-soaked voice sounding sultry and sexy in the night. In her right hand she gripped a five Euro bottle of Chianti which she raised as an enticement, like she required an enticement with those eyes and everything that went with those eyes. "Look, Chase. I brought refreshments."

I felt my heart beating. Felt my blood flowing through my veins. I glanced down at Lulu who was standing just a couple of feet away on the smooth wood floor of my five-hundred-year-old third-floor apartment.

"What should I do, Lu?" I whispered.

"You know what you should do," the pit bull said with a wag of her tail. "You should go the hell back to bed. Get up bright and early in the morning, work

on your new book, then get in a quick run before having to meet your group at ten for the Duomo tour. That's what you should do. Don't forget, you need the dough-ray-mi."

"Yah," I agreed, gazing back down onto the blonde goddess dressed in short black mini-skirt, black lace tights and knee-length leather boots. "I should go back to bed, shouldn't I?"

"But you're not going to do that are you, Chase?" Lu added. "As usual you're gonna listen to your dick, unlock the door for this lonely but very married tourist, invite her into your world. You're gonna drink her wine until it's almost gone and then you're gonna get naked. From that point on I gotta be forced to listen to your moans and groans and bed-board banging when I should be getting my rest. But then, what the hell do I know? I'm just a stupid dog. I don't even know I'm alive."

"You sure you're just a dog, Lu?"

"If it looks like a dog, smells like a dog, barks like a dog..."

"Most dogs don't talk human speak."

"Most dogs ain't gotta live with you, Chase. And you're making all this dialogue up in your head anyway."

"Thanks for reminding me, Lu. Thought I finally lost it for a minute."

Working up a grin, I inhaled a deep, satisfying breath, and decided, "What the hell?"

That's when I proceeded to jump down into the rabbit hole.

"Okay, Mrs. Doyle, I'm gonna let you in. But just for an hour. Long day tomorrow, remember? The Duomo tour and the 'David' in the Academia. You're paying me big bucks for this."

"Oh, good one, Chase." Lu, moaning under her breath. "Real smooth."

"Back off, Lu. Daddy's got a date." A wide smile plastered on my face, I sprinted out of the bedroom to the front door. Unbolting the door, I leaped down the stairs to let her in...

...Ten hours, thirty-three minutes, and sixteen seconds later, I find myself wrestling. Only I'm not naked and the person I'm wrestling with is most

definitely not a jade-eyed blonde *beauty. I'm grappling with the overweight husband of said jade-eyed beauty.*

A one, Mr. Robert Doyle.

"I knew you were with her last night when I rolled over and she was gone," screams the red-faced faced man, as he tries to trap me in a bear hug. "I knew it the moment you set eyes on her you'd try and get in her pants."

I shove the far softer Doyle away, hold up my hands in surrender like I want no part of fighting him. And I don't. He's my client after all, and by the looks of his physical constitution, only two heartbeats away from a major coronary.

"She came to me, Mr. Doyle. Last night at midnight when I was asleep."

"That supposed to make me feel better, Chase Baker?"

In the near distance, the wailing sirens growing louder. So is the crowd that surrounds me.

"Fight!" someone barks. An Australian. "Don't just dance like a couple of Sallies."

Australians love to fight.

"Yah, punch his lights outs!" someone else shouts. A Japanese man. Sounds like, "Punch his whites out!"

But I really don't want to go all Russell Crowe on this man; don't want to punch his lights out. He's just angry, confused and hurt.

Doyle takes another swing at me, and another. This time he connects with my right jaw, sending a shock wave of pain into my head. It also flicks a trigger. My defensive trigger. The one that brings out Chase Baker the Survivor. The one that's been triggered in bars and Irish pubs the world over. Istanbul, Athens, Cairo, Rome. You name it. I've tossed my fair share of punches and swallowed a few too. But this is the first time it's happened while working.

"Chase, don't you dare hurt my husband!" cries the suddenly concerned voice of Mrs. Doyle. She's still looking mighty choice in her black mini skirt and leather boots. She did her share of screaming last night in my apartment. Now she's screaming once

more. Only difference is, she's changed her tune entirely. Her eyes are filled with tears and she's clutching her face with her pretty little hands. I'm the bad guy now. Like last night's little midnight affair was all my idea.

"Don't you dare hurt my husband, you big bully!"

Her face is a combination remorse, fear and hatred for herself over what she's done.

I know the look all too well. I've seen that face before on a dozen other too-attractive-for-their-own-good girls whose husbands have just discovered the worst thing they can possibly imagine: That their pretty little trophy wives are also pretty little cheats.

My head is ringing like the Duomo bell. I feel slightly out of balance. So much so that I don't see yet another punch coming. This one connects with my other jaw. The crowd roars in approval.

If the first wallop triggered a survival mechanism, this one sparks rage.

"Sorry, Mr. Doyle," I say, "but you leave me little choice."

Taking a step into the bigger man's body, I lead

with an uppercut that travels through the math teacher's soft underbelly all the way to his spine. I then quickly follow up with a left hook to the lower jaw and just like that, it's lights out for Mr. Doyle on the cobblestones of a breathtaking Renaissance treasure.

It's also precisely when the polizia arrive.

They jump out of their white and blue Fiat squad car, grab me by my weight-trained arms, demand that I drop to my knees. How's the old saying go? It's not the angry man who punches first who gets caught. It's the sucker who punches last who eats the crap sandwich.

"Hey, he started it!" I shout. But what I really should be doing is pointing at Mrs. Doyle, insisting, she started it!

The polizia don't want to hear it anyway. This isn't the first time they've picked me up for brawling and it certainly won't be the last. They push my arms up over my head in the opposite way God intended for them to be pushed. The pain causes little flashes of white light to explode in my brain as I feel the steel cuffs being slapped over my wrists.

"You big bully!" shouts Mrs. Doyle as she slaps me across the face. Then, dropping to her knees over her out-cold husband, "Oh my sweet darling, are you okay?"

"Let's go, Chase," one of the blue-uniformed cops insists in his Italian-accented English. "You've got yourself a front row audience with Detective Cipriani...Vai, vai."

"Does this mean I'm under arrest, officer?" I say as they painfully yank me up onto my feet.

"Si," the other cop says. "It means your ass is glass."

"Grass," I say. "It's 'ass is grass.' Why don't you learn to get it right, Pinocchio?"

I feel the quick fist to the gut, and it's all I can do not to double over.

"Why don't you learn to shut up, Chase?" the cop says. "Silencio."

"Good idea," I say through gritting teeth. "I should learn to shut up and you should learn to speak English...The international language of choice the

world over."

Together the cops drag me to the squad car where they thrust me into the back seat, slamming the door closed. An EMT van arrives on the scene then, the medical technicians immediately exiting the vehicle and going to work on the still prone Doyle. Meanwhile, the cops hop back into the front of the cruiser.

As the cop behind the wheel pulls away from the piazza, I catch one more glimpse of Mrs. Doyle. She's still kneeling over her husband. I shoot her a smile, like, Thanks for last night. But she returns my glance with a glare that would ice over Dante's Inferno. When she raises up her right hand and flips me a manicured middle finger, I realize I should have listened to my dog, Lu, and not my other head.

"I'll never learn," I whisper to yourself. "Oh well, at least Detective Cipriani has nice cigars."

I contemplate smoking a fine Cuban cigar all the way to polizia headquarters.

VINCENT ZANDRI

1

"Signor Chase Baker!" shouts the guard sergeant as he approaches the iron bars of this dark, dank, basement holding cell. "You are free to go! Andare!"

I shove through a pen that's filled mostly with drunk, piss-soaked vagrants who've migrated from Peru. Why they cross over the big drink to Italy instead of heading north to America, which is far closer, beats the hell out of me. Maybe they get better health care here. Or maybe it has something to do with a higher alcohol content in the beer…Yeah that's it, more alcohol in the beer.

The barred door slides open.

I step on through, offer the uniformed guard sergeant a smile like, *Top o' the mornin' to ya!* Or, *Top o' the late afternoon anyway.* He doesn't smile back. Go figure.

"Su," he says, nodding at the staircase before me.

Su…That's Italian for "up." As in, *Get the hell up those stairs!* It's also something an American redneck might shout at an old dog before kicking it in the ass with his Redwing-booted foot.

"Up the stairs, Chase. Detective Cipriani would like a word with you in his office."

"He asking or telling?" I say.

But the short, stocky cop just glares at me like he has no idea how to answer my query. And he doesn't. The guard sergeant on my heels, I climb the concrete steps as ordered, like an old dog being led around by his master.

A minute later I'm granted my private audience with Florence's top cop. If you want to call him that. Detective Federico Cipriani closes the door to his office, asks me to take a seat in a wood chair set before his long dark wood desk. Set out on the desktop is a translucent plastic baggy that contains my personals: my belt, the laces to my boots, my wallet, my passport, my cell phone, my cigs, my Saint Christopher's medal, my gun, my bullets … I go to reach for them.

"Not yet!" barks Cipriani, from across the room. "We need to talk first, Chase."

I sit back, my eyes peeled on the internationally licensed 9 mm Smith & Wesson.

"Looks like the Doyles aren't pressing charges," I say. "How sweet of them."

The fifty-something Cipriani goes behind his desk, sits himself down. He's a big man with a barrel chest and a pleasant looking face mostly hidden behind a thick but well-trimmed beard. His eyes are brown as is his hair, and the dark blue suit he wears was no doubt purchased in Florence, probably at the department store across the street from the Piazza Della Republica.

"It's true they have dropped their case of assault against you," he nods, picking up my handgun, staring down contemplatively at it. "But that doesn't excuse you from punching the merda out of an American tourist."

"You detaining me further, Cip?" I say, pronouncing the nickname like "Chip."

He shakes his head.

"No, just trying to somehow get it through that thick skull of yours that the time will come when I can no longer keep you out of trouble. Eventually you will be asked to leave Italy for good."

I force my eyes wide open.

"Never," I say. "Who will guide all those lovely lost women who've just arrived from America and England and Australia and Japan and China and Russia and…?"

"I'll never understand it why a bestselling author like you still insists on providing guided tours or working as a private detective or even a, what do you call it, sand dog? Doesn't make sense."

"Three reasons," I say, slipping my hand inside my bush jacket for my cigarettes, but then quickly realizing that they are stuffed into the plastic bag along with my lighter and my bullets. Oh well, I've been trying to quit on and off for years now. "One, writing is a solitary existence. It gets mighty lonely. Second, guiding, detecting and sand*hogging*—not sandhogging—provides me with badly needed human contact and it also makes for good story material now and again. Third, the money is good and on occasion great. Royalties are good too but not always so consistent. You with me here, Cip? Just think of me as a Renaissance man living and thriving in the home of the Renaissance."

He spins the gun on his thick index finger like a little boy and his plastic six-shooter, bites down on his lip.

"You know I don't like that you are able to carry this in my peaceful town of art and culture."

"Money talks," I smile. "Especially in Italy. Just ask the American GIs who saved your ass from Nazi enslavement during World War Two. And you personally signed off on my permit, don't forget. Besides, this isn't your town anyway, Cip. It's Brunelleschi's town, or haven't you noticed that big giant marble dome occupying the center of the city?"

"You're not getting any younger, Chase. Soon you will not be so attractive to the young women who travel to this beautiful country. Perhaps you will now consider spending more time with your daughter in

New York City." Working up a smile. "You know, grow old gracefully. With dignity."

"The food is better here. So is the wine. And I'm forty something. I'm not even close to old, yet."

Cip sets the gun down on top of his desk. Opening the small wooden box set beside it, he pulls out a cigar, cuts the tip off with a small metal device he produces from his jacket pocket and gently sets it between his front upper and bottom teeth. Firing the cigar up with a silver-plated Zippo, he sensually releases a cloud of blue smoke through puckered lips. Then, slowly straightening himself up in his swivel chair, he reaches across the desk with his free hand, pushes the box of cigars in my direction.

"Thought you'd never ask," I say.

Stealing a cigar from the box, I bite off the tip, spit it onto the wood floor. Leaning over the desk, I allow the cop to light me up.

"You always were a class act, Cip," I say, sitting back. "When do I get my gun back?"

"Not yet," he says. "I have a favor to ask of you first."

I exhale the good tasting and very smooth Cuban-born smoke. If silence were golden, we'd be bathing in the stuff.

Finally, I say, "Okay, Cip, you've got that look on your face like we're going to be working together again whether I like it or not. What do you need? You want me to dig up some dirt on someone? Maybe follow some cheating hubby around Flo for a while?"

He shakes his head, smokes.

"Not exactly," he explains. "But you're right. It's possible I have a job for you."

"I'm listening, so long as it pays."

He gets up, comes around the desk, approaches the set of French windows behind me, opens them onto the noises of the old city.

"I need you to find a missing man for me," he says after a time.

I turn in my seat, looking at his backside as he faces out onto the cobbled street below.

"Find him where?" I say, knowing the question sounds like a silly one since if Cip knew where the man was he wouldn't be asking me to find him in the first place. But it's a good place to start.

"Somewhere in the Middle East would be my best guess. Egypt, perhaps."

I smoke a little, visions of my sandhogging days in and around the Giza Plateau pulsing in my brain.

"Egypt," I repeat. "Not the safest of places at this point in modern global history."

"Especially if you're an American. And the man I want you to find is indeed an American."

"What's his name?"

Cip backs away from the window, returns to his desk. Only instead of reclaiming his place behind it, he takes a seat on the desk's edge, left foot dangling off the edge, the right foot planted.

"His name is Dr. Andre Manion. A biblical archeology professor from a small Catholic college in your Midwest. An expert on the historical Jesus of Nazareth and said to have discovered some relics belonging to the Jesus family."

The name strikes home. So much so that a lesser man would allow the small electrical shock of the name to show on his face. But I'm not a lesser man.

Or so I pretend.

"Did you say relics? Jesus relics?"

"Yes, I did. Priceless antiquities, which no doubt stir your juices, perhaps more than Mr. Doyle's wife did last evening. Manion's over here on a teaching sabbatical at the American University. Or supposed to be here teaching, I should say. Early last month he went missing and hasn't been seen or heard from since."

Cip is right. The name Manion when combined with relics and antiquities does indeed stir my juices.

"Fact of the matter is this, Cip: I worked as a sandhog for Manion eight years ago in and around Giza where we were in search of some prized Biblical treasures. Perhaps the most prized Biblical treasure of all. But we never did find much of anything, and truth is, Manion ran out on me, leaving me hopelessly hungover and alone."

"Sounds very dramatic, Chase," Cip smiles. "I thank you for your honesty."

"Don't mention it. Obviously, my life has improved in leaps and bounds since those days."

"Obviously," Cip says. "That prize fight performance in the Piazza Del Duomo is proof of that."

"Very funny," I say. Then, "Thought you said Manion was in Egypt?"

"That's the best possible guess based upon what we've put together thus far. I didn't say there weren't any clues as to his specific whereabouts inside the embattled country. I said he himself hasn't been seen, other than on airport security video in both the Florence and Cairo airports."

"He traveling alone?"

"Don't know the answer to that."

"Exactly what relics has Manion uncovered?"

I feel my heart race as I ask the question.

"Don't know the answer to that either," he admits. "But I've heard a rumor that he uncovered the small tomb that housed the bones of Joseph, Jesus's father. But that was a while ago now and, in any case, finds of this magnitude would naturally be snatched up by the Vatican. That is, the finds can be verified in the first place. Naturally you would be familiar with such a process."

"Naturally," I say. "Or at the very least, the relics would go to the highest bidding private collector. Perhaps someone from Moscow. Or maybe one of your richer-than-God friends in Florence, Cip."

The top cop smokes, glares at me for a moment, like he's waiting for the stink from my comment to dissipate.

I add, "I assume your support staff has done everything in their power to locate him?"

"And then some. We've even gotten Interpol involved. But they, too, have come up short. Egypt is not the most cooperative of countries since its revolution and the election of a radical Islamist-backed government."

I reach into the right-hand pocket of my bush jacket, pull out a small notebook and a Bic ballpoint that Short, Stocky Guard Sergeant failed to relieve me of before tossing me into the pen with the drunk Peruvians. I click on the back of the pen with my thumb, jot down the name Manion, as if I need to. Then I write the name, Jesus, as if I need to do that also. Finally, I scribble in a dollar sign, just for good measure. Makes me smile when I look at it.

"Manion got a wife? A mother? A boyfriend? Someone I can speak with who might help me out here?"

I can't recall if the professor was married at the time we were digging all over Egypt. I recall him mentioning a woman now and again. But I don't recall her name.

"His wife is in town. She teaches English at the same college her husband teaches at. She's been here for a couple of weeks now. She desperately wants to find him. In the meantime, she can be a wealth of information for you, if you play her the right way and keep your dick in your pants."

"Hey, you know me," I smile.

"That's what I'm afraid of."

"Who would I be working for? You or her?"

"If you take the job, you'll be working directly for her. She's independently wealthy I'm told."

"My kind of client."

He slides off his desk, goes around it to his top

drawer, which he pulls open. He slides out a manila envelope and tosses it across the desk so that it lands on the desk's edge. I take the package in hand and go to open it when he stops me.

"Take it home," he insists. "Examine it. Take your time. You should know that this one won't be easy. It will also be dangerous."

"You mean I can actually say no for a change?"

"Sure you can, Chase. Under one condition."

"And that is?"

"You pack up and head back home to the states, since I will personally revoke your temporary work permit and your permit to carry a firearm in Italy."

"Those are my choices?"

"Take them or leave them."

I smoke and pretend to think about taking the job.

"Can you perhaps give me a hint about what it is Manion was working on and why he was willing to disappear in order to find it?"

But then, I already know precisely what he's working on. I just want to hear it from the good detective's smoky mouth.

"My guess is that Manion is being paid by a private investor to locate something of extreme sensitivity in religious circles."

"Which means it would be worth a lot of money in people circles," I say, my eyes no doubt, lit up like the lights on a Christmas tree.

"Watch yourself, Chase," Cip warns. "If what Manion is in search of is as important as I think it is, more than one person will be willing to die in order to get their hands on it."

I feel the weight of the package in my hands.

"What the hell is Manion after, Cip?"

I need to hear it, to believe it …

Exhaling, he says, "I don't know for sure since you will have to speak to his wife. But it's possible that the professor has stumbled upon something that is liable to shake up the very foundation of Christian belief as the world knows it."

The words aren't exactly what I want to hear, but on the other hand, the words can only mean one thing. I stand up, my head feeling a little lightheaded from the cigar and from what Cip is telling me.

"And that is?" I press.

"The bones of Jesus himself."

There, he said it. Said what I wanted him to say.

For the love of God, the quest for the mortal remains of Jesus begins again.

VINCENT ZANDRI

2

I grew up with Jesus. The product of a Catholic school guarded by yard-stick wielding nuns who could make the toughest of corrections officers look namby-pamby, I grew up fearing the big guy. My mother and father might have feared him too, but they were nonetheless devoutly, overtly and hopelessly Catholic.

My father, at one time, considered becoming a priest. But I think he knew deep inside he could never be married to a faith, despite its impenetrable strength. A faith could never bear children, for instance. No way faith could bring in the big bucks like excavation contracting and sandhogging all over the globe could. So, instead of donning a stiff white collar and a black suit, my dad operated a backhoe, managed a shoveling crew, and he made money.

My mother bore me and two older sisters whom I no longer kept in touch with once our parents were dead, buried, and seated beside the Lord they so revered. I don't think of my family all too often. Try not to dwell on where I came from and how I made my way out of its confines. But I do sometimes find myself thinking of Jesus … The historical Jesus of Nazareth.

I have no doubt that he once existed. That he must have been a great man and a powerful presence for him to be remembered so precisely, with such reverence and acclaim. Religions have been created in his name and many wars have been fought over his beliefs or, the beliefs mortal man have attributed to him. I fought in two of those wars in both Iraq and in Afghanistan. The wars were about the control of oil, but they were also about radical Muslims versus Judeo/Christians.

As I walk back toward my apartment across the Piazza Santa Maria Novella, I picture the long-haired man of legend being lashed by Roman soldiers while down on his knees, a crown of sharp thorns piercing his forehead, the blood streaking down an anguished face. I picture him walking the narrow cobbled streets of Jerusalem, a heavy cross bearing down upon his shoulder, he dropping to his knees under the heavy burden. I picture him being nailed to that cross on an ugly rock-strewn quarry called Golgotha or Skull Place and which is located just outside the city walls, the cross being raised slowly by the scarlet-robed soldiers, until the heavy vertical beam dropped down in place, his body falling hard against the nails that pierced both flesh and bone.

Is it possible that Manion is finally on the true trail of the Jesus Remains?

Walking the cobbled streets of a Medieval city filled with churches and cathedrals honoring Jesus's name, I can help but imagine the enormous sum of cash the true bones of Christ would fetch on the private collector's market. If Rupert Murdoch is willing to pay $100 million for the bones of Richard III, might he not be willing to scrounge up $500 million or even a billion for the remains of the Son of Man?

Listen, I might get hot and bothered by the thought of digging up that kind of relic, but I firmly believe they belong in a museum to be studied and pondered by scholars for eons to come. However, I wouldn't be averse from taking a few million for my efforts should I happen to come upon them during my search for Manion.

Why?

Bestselling author or not, the truth of the matter is this: My finances are in shambles. As of late, neither my books nor any one of my other occupations are making me any money. As for sandhogging, that job dried up eight years ago in the hot Giza sand when Manion ditched me for a plane back to the U.S. I don't live in Florence because I love it. I live there because the lease on my downtown Manhattan apartment is about to be terminated due to unpaid rents.

You might also recall Detective Cipriani mentioning the fact that I have a daughter. That's right. Chase Baker, free spirit, bon vivant, and all-around Renaissance man is a dad.

Maybe finding adventures and writing fictions

based upon them has become a passion for me. But my eight-year-old, long brunette-haired, brown-eyed daughter, Ava, is the love of my life. Problem is, I've fallen so far behind on the support payments that no way I can fly to the states and not expect to be slapped with an injunction as soon as I get off the plane. If I'm ever to see my little baby again, I'll have to make good on all my debts before I leave Italian soil. That means a substantial, if not huge, payday.

Perhaps having stumbled onto the job of finding Manion is the best luck I've had in a long time. That in mind, I climb the stone stairs to my apartment, knowing that gripped in my hand is not just a packet of information about an archeology professor who's gone missing in the pursuit of Jesus.

It just might also be my ticket back home.

My ticket back to Ava.

VINCENT ZANDRI

3

Lulu greets me as soon as I come through the door. Which tells me she's snuck into the main apartment from her bed out on the terracotta-covered terrace via the open window that accesses the dining room. My fault for leaving it open. The small but muscle-bound dog jumps and yelps until I pick her solid body up in my arms and hold her for a minute or two. Then, letting her back down, I make up a bowl of the dry dog food she eats for breakfast, lunch and dinner, and set it onto the kitchen floor. I grab a cold Moretti beer from the fridge and sit down at a breakfast counter that abuts a set of tall French doors leading out onto the grape vine-covered terrace.

Opening the package, I slide out the materials it contains. Not much in the way of information. A couple of eight-by-ten color glossies of Manion.

He's the man I remember. Tall, salt and pepper-haired, professorial-looking. His long face is clean shaven, his cheeks sunken in a bit, lips thin and uninteresting, as are his eyes which are brown and neither large nor deeply set.

If I didn't already know that he is an archeologist I would peg him for an accountant, or maybe a department store manager. In the photo he's teaching a class, his right hand extended up at a blackboard upon which a diagram has been drawn. If I have to guess, the diagram represents a crypt of some kind. An ancient, ornate burial chamber. I've seen the real thing plenty of times before.

In the second photo, the professor is shown working an archeology dig. I can't be sure, but it looks like he's in Israel. I've dug in the Jewish state on several occasions and I recognize the unique way the sun shines down on that porous, almost hospital white rock. In the photo, the tall, gawky Manion is wearing khaki clothing and a baseball hat with cloth flaps hanging down from it in order to protect the exposed skin on his neck. If I remember correctly, the world-class archeologist has a problem with sunburn. Being of Mediterranean descent, the hot sun doesn't bother me. Even equatorial sun. It just makes me bronze. My good luck. Good luck for the ladies too.

Setting the photos back down, I grab the vital stat sheet Cip provided for me which is typed out on Florence Polizia letterhead.

Manion, Andre, PhD—Archeology/Psychology, University of Chicago, 1982, University of Chicago, 1984

Height: 6'1"

Color: Caucasian.

DOB: Feb 23, 1964

Status: Separated/Divorced

I set the paper back down.

"So, check this out, Lu," I say. "Manion isn't just an archeologist. He's also a shrink. Funny combination. Never knew that about him."

Lu looks up at me from her food dish.

"Who's Manion?"

"Oh, I forgot to tell you. Manion is our meal ticket

home. He's apparently gone missing in the desert. Probably outside Cairo where he's working on digging up the bones of Jesus and who knows what else. I worked with him once before, until he ran out on the dig and me."

"Jesus … You mean the Jesus Died-On-The-Cross-For-Our-Sins Christ?"

"The one and only. What's important is that if I find Manion, I just might get a chance at digging up a few treasures of my own. Or perhaps even assisting in acquiring the very relic Manion is looking for. What a payday that would bring in my canine friend."

Lu coughs something up into her mouth, then swallows whatever it is.

"Isn't that stealing?" she asks.

"No. Errr, yes. But not like stealing in the classical sense. If those unearthed relics are truly up for grabs then it's first come, first serve. That's the law of the desert and the law of tomb raiding. But I am a little confused about one thing: the Professor Manion I once knew would never think of selling out to a private collector. But, from the looks of it, somebody's financing his new dig and that somebody has enough money to not only lure him away from his teaching gig in Florence, but also to simply render himself legally missing."

"Sounds dangerous. Jesus is one important human."

"In human terms, perhaps the most important man who ever lived."

"Then it stands to reason that if this Manion guy is about to locate his mortal body, a lot of people are going to want to have at it. Maybe even be willing to kill for it. You still got a gun, Chase?"

I drink some beer, pat my left rib cage upon which hangs my newly liberated 9 mm.

"As always, Lu."

"Where you gonna start looking?"

"Not sure. I need to speak to Manion's estranged wife first since she's the one financing the search. Word up is she's in town already. So, I guess you could say my search starts right here in Flo."

"Be careful, and remember, you're talking to a

dog here."

"Thanks Lu. I trust you won't tell anyone about our conversations."

"That would be up to you since you're the one making this shit up."

"Duly noted."

The last items contained in the package are several newspaper clippings.

The first one is lifted from the *New York Times* and it's dated February 2002. It shows Manion standing before what I immediately recognize as an ossuary, which is nothing more than a square shaped box carved out of sandstone. It's about the size of a banker's box and the lid is gable-shaped. The headline on the piece reads, **Bones of Jesus' Stepfather Found?**

The article describes the controversial discovery of a box on the Israel side of the Sinai which supposedly contains the bones of Joseph, Jesus's father and husband to the Virgin Mary. The article states that the ossuary has been carbon dated back to the early first century and contains both Aramaic and

Latin text of the time. According to Manion, the inscription of the box reads, "Here lies the body of Joseph, father of Jesus and James, husband of Mary." Naysayers, however, say that the bones could belong to anyone since the names Joseph, Mary, James, and even Jesus, were very common in those days.

"I guess the court is still out on that one," I whisper to myself. "But then, how many men actually had sons named Jesus and James while being married to a Mary, way back in first century Palestine? Couldn't have been all that many."

I'm still contemplating the Joseph ossuary when my doorbell rings.

Setting down the article, I slide off the stool, head out of the kitchen, through the dining room which also serves as my writing room. Past the library and its bookshelves, and relic-covered walls, past the living room and its high, wood-beamed ceiling and finally to the stone-covered vestibule.

Unlocking the deadbolt, I open the wood door to a woman. A tall, very well-built woman of maybe forty, with short light brown hair and deep blue eyes.

She's wearing a black turtleneck sweater, black jeans and black, lace-up boots. She's also wearing a matching leather jacket. Strapped over her shoulder is a bag, also made of leather, and perhaps purchased in the Florence leather markets. The kind of bag I might store a manuscript in.

"Mr. Chase Baker?" she says, her eyes wide, her bottom lip trembling just slightly. "I hope I'm not intruding."

I have to force myself to peel my eyes off her. But me, being me, it isn't easy.

"Can I help you with something, lady? I'm working."

Lu scrambles up beside me, pressing her muscular body against my shin. She growls which catches me a bit by surprise. Lu usually loves people. Even strangers.

"It's okay, Lu," I say.

The woman catches sight of the pit bull, takes a tentative step back. She tries working up a smile. But it's obvious the dog is making her uncomfortable. Or maybe it's me who's making her nervous.

She says, "I thought Detective Cipriani would have told you I was coming?"

I shake my head.

"Must have slipped his mind. Who are you and what are you doing on my doorstep?"

"Do you always act this tough?"

"Only around beautiful women who come calling unannounced."

"Maybe I should introduce myself," she says, reaching out and gently touching my arm. "I'm Mrs. Andre Manion. It's my husband who's gone missing."

I stare down at her hand.

"Your husband?"

"Correction," she exhales, gently retreating her hand. "Ex-husband."

"So I hear," I say, still playing it cool despite her luscious eyes. "And what would you like me to do about it?"

"I want you to find him."

"And then what?"

"Bring him back alive," she says.

VINCENT ZANDRI

4

She enters the apartment, her shoulder brushing against mine as she walks past. Setting her bag on the couch, she gives the place the once over.

"Looks like a museum," she laughs. Then, turning to me, "If you're making coffee, I'd love some."

"Is that an order?" I say, playing hard to get. "Because if it is, I haven't agreed to taking on this job. Looks dangerous enough for me to lose my skin. And I like my skin. It fits nice."

By all appearances she has no idea about my history with her husband, and that's the way I want to keep it, at least for the moment. If she knows I went after the Jesus bones with him once before and he had cause to run out on me, no way in hell will she tolerate me getting a second chance to make a grab for them. She'll just assume I'm some sort of opportunistic grave robber looking to make a quick buck. And the hell of it is, she'd be right.

"That's not your reputation, Mr. Chase Baker," she says. "I'm told you are quite handy around an archeology dig and even handier when it comes to finding a missing person. Both in real life and in your novels."

"You've read my books." It's a question.

"All three of them. *Deception* was my favorite. I loved how the detective deciphered clues only by looking at their reflection in a special hand-held mirror. Clever. Even your prose was passable. I teach English, you know."

"The mirror was the book's hook, Ms. English Prof."

"Indeed, and it's a good one. It's almost like you took it from real life."

"Maybe I did. But how do I know you're not just trying to butter me up here?"

She cocks her head, which admittedly, is a very pretty head, then bites down gently on her bottom lip.

"I have no reason to compliment you on your

work. If I want something from you, I will ask you directly."

"So why not just ask me politely to help you find your husband?"

She smiles.

"I already have, and so has the detective. I've just come to confirm the status of your employment."

The room falls silent on us, on the many books, on the many pieces of treasure I've accumulated over the years in Europe, the Middle East, South America and God knows where else. Skulls, amulets, statuettes, rocks, jars of ashes, and a mirror. A special mirror about the size of a credit card and almost as thin. A mirror that's broken in half and that I dug up inside a deep pit outside the Third Pyramid within the Giza Plateau back when I was sandhogging for Manion … But that's only for me to know.

"Think I'll make some coffee," I say, heading into the kitchen.

Pulling down the stove-top coffee pot from the shelf over the sink, I fill the bottom with tap water, and the coffee receptacle with Lavazza espresso. I light the gas stove, set the pot on the burner and wait for the magic to happen. When it does three minutes later, I pour the coffee into an espresso cup, grab hold of my already open beer, and carry them back out to the living room.

I find her standing, facing my floor-to-ceiling shelves, gazing upon the books and relics.

"You have quite the collection," she says. "You remind me of the most interesting man in the world … a real Renaissance man."

"I've heard a lot of women call me a lot of things. But never that." I hand her the coffee. Then, "So, Mrs. Manion, remind me of your given name again."

She turns to me, carefully sipping her coffee.

"My first name," she says. "It's Anya."

"Anya and Andre," I say. "How cute."

"We were a cute couple. Very much in love. A long, long time ago."

"Now you are divorcing. Or already divorced."

She nods, sadly.

"My husband has been carrying on an affair for a long time, Mr. Chase—"

"—Just Chase."

"Thank you, Renaissance man, Chase Baker …
Anyway, my husband has been carrying on an affair
that has become his obsession."

"I'm sorry to hear that," I say, visions of the many
women who have come through this door over the
years, their husbands still waiting for them unawares
back in their hotel room. "Seems like nothing is
sacred when it comes to marriage these days."

She shakes her head vehemently.

"You don't understand," she adds. "If my
husband were to have an affair with another woman,
that would be one thing. We might be able to work
that out and start over. But this one is different."

"I'm not following," I say, taking a swig of beer.

She sips her coffee, comes up for air.

"My husband is not carrying on an affair with a
woman."

"Oh, I'm sorry," I say. "He's switched teams."

"No," she laughs. "I could deal easily enough with
that too."

"Okay, Anya, let's have it. Who is your missing

husband seeing behind your back?"

She finishes her coffee, sets the cup down onto the wood coffee table, straightens up, crossing her arms over her chest.

"He's carrying on an affair with Jesus," she says. "And that's why I've left him."

I finish my beer, go grab another one, take it back with me into the living room.

"Let me get this straight," I say. "You left your husband because he's overly obsessed with finding the bones of Jesus. Yet here you are standing in my living room asking me to find him? Why not just let him go and get on with his obsession? Live your life? Teach your English classes?"

Her face takes on a pained expression. Like the coffee I just served her is making her sick. She gently sits herself down onto the couch.

"I didn't say I don't love Andre, Chase," she says. "Love *and* care about him. All I said is that our marriage is over."

"But you still want me to find him for you?"

"I'm worried about him. About his ... let's say

health."

"Why not leave it to the police? To Interpol? Doesn't make sense to pay me when they can do it for free."

Me, still playing hard to get. To perhaps up my price. Maybe considerably so.

"No," she says. "I would prefer to keep the police out of the loop as much as possible. Andre's work is very sensitive."

"So are the people he's working for, no doubt."

She stares at the wood plank floor.

"Yes," she says. "It's possible that if the police were to become involved by making themselves plainly visible, grave harm could come to my husband."

"Better to hire me and put my head on the chopping block," I say. "I don't come cheap. Neither does my head."

She says nothing for a heavily weighted moment. Just as well. I use the time to drink a little more beer. It's while drinking the beer that it hits me. Professor Manion didn't just get up one morning, get dressed, head to the airport and fly away on his own. He had a little help in the matter.

"Anya," I say. "Is it possible your husband was kidnaped?"

She looks at me hard. Not at me, but into me.

"It's not only possible, Renaissance Man," she sighs. "It's the sad truth."

5

"I'm gonna come clean," I say, straightening out the shoulder strap on my black, Tough Traveler writing satchel. "I know your husband. Or, used to know him. I worked as a sandhog for him eight years ago in the Giza Plateau."

"I had no idea," she says, shooting me a look of suspicion. But I'm listening to my insides and they are telling me she could be putting on an act. "Why did you wait until now to tell me?"

"I didn't want you to think I'm some opportunist who wants to find your husband only to ultimately find the treasure he's no doubt seeking."

She works up a grin that makes me want to press my lips against hers. But not yet.

"Seems strange you not knowing about my past relationship with your husband," I say, recalling my conversation with Cipriani. "You just happen to call on the one man in all of Florence to try and find your husband and it turns out I'm very familiar with him."

"Stranger things have happened, Renaissance Man," she says, brushing back her lush hair with her hands. "Do you still want the job?"

"Give me the rest of the truth," I say, shifting the weight of my satchel over my shoulder. "Straight, no bullshit."

The apartment has grown too cramped, too tense. What I want is for Anya to tell me everything about her husband … everything I don't already know, that is … and do so over a drink at a nice quiet bar down the road in the less touristy Via Guelfa, American University area not far from where Manion was supposed to be teaching. It's precisely why I've put Lu back outside on the terrace and locked up the apartment.

Now walking side by side on the cobbled Via Guelfa, Anya goes on with her story: "My husband has been researching the remains of Jesus and his family for years. Most people, including scholars thought him crazy. Because even if the remains somehow exist, it's likely they would never be found. The desert, even around the Giza plateau, is just too massive. Or perhaps they've already been found and now reside in a secret chamber in the Vatican. Or perhaps they have turned to dust like so many ancient bones. But then Andre found the Joseph remains, and the world took notice. So did the church. From there on in, the greater possibility that Christ's bones could be found, took on a greater reality."

I'm aware of most of this. It was what attracted me to Andre in the first place in the early years of the new century. Not only his knowledge about the possible resting place of the Jesus remains, but his utter belief in their existence.

Up ahead is the DaVinci Bar. The exposed brick building is mostly frequented by art students and professors drinking coffee and smoking cigarettes. It's also quiet, dark and cavernous enough that we can talk in privacy while fading into the far shadows.

We enter and take a table in back. Setting my satchel onto the table, I go to the bar, retrieve us both a glass of vino rosso a piece. I bring the wine back with me to the table, set it down and sit across from her.

"But I thought the Joseph bones were found to be frauds," I say, continuing where we left off. "You telling me the Joseph bones were real?"

"The Vatican did it's best to debunk them," she says. "And the media sided with the Pope. But Andre knew different. He knew he was on the trail of finding Jesus now that he had Joseph's bones and evidence of a Jesus family crypt outside the Jerusalem walls. He was also gathering the attention of some pretty serious investors, which made him nervous, of course."

"Such as?"

"One man in particular. A wealthy Egyptian from Cairo and a friend of their new, rather radical President."

"What's his name?"

"That's just it. I don't know his name because he never would tell me. Something about the less I knew the healthier it would be for the both of us. But I do know this: The wealthy man is an oil tycoon by trade and in the possession of infinite resources."

"Do you think it's possible he is the one who kidnaped Andre?"

She sips her wine. Nods.

"You have to ask? The wealthy man is no doubt a part of the Muslim Brotherhood which worked so hard to push their party into absolute power after a revolution which promised freedom."

"I don't get it," I say. "Why would a Muslim be interested in Jesus?"

"Power," she says. "The ultimate act of crushing the Roman Catholic Church and tipping western belief onto its side."

I steal a sip of wine. I also take a look over my right shoulder at the small crowd gathered around the half dozen tables that fill the place. At one of the tables near the front entrance sits a solitary man. Not an unusual situation for this place. A dark-haired man, with a salt and pepper beard, black leather coat, reading glasses. He's gazing at a newspaper. *The Florentine*. Florence's English newspaper. Probably a professor, if I had to guess. No doubt from the same school where Andre was teaching before his abduction.

I turn back to Anya.

"I'm still not making the connection between the bones of Christ and the Muslim Brotherhood, other than their tremendous monetary value to the right investor."

She straightens herself up, runs her hand through her thick hair.

"Don't you see, Chase?" she says. "Islam reveres Jesus. They believe him to be a great miracle maker. The Koran speaks almost as highly of Jesus as they do Mohamed. But they also believe in something that the Vatican would rather we not know about."

"And that is?"

"They believe that the man crucified on the cross somewhere around 30 A.D. was not Jesus, but a double. A fill-in if you will. They believe that the disciples protected the real Jesus and slipped him out of Jerusalem to protect him from his enemies."

"The Jewish Sanhedrin and the Romans."

"Once he was condemned and put to death, the movement Jesus started would be over. That's the way the Sanhedrin and the Romans saw it anyway. That way they could maintain their way of life. All self-proclaimed Messiahs were dealt with this way. But, Jesus of Nazareth was different. He wasn't a quack screaming his head off about doom's day. He was the real deal."

"A real threat, in other words."

I feel something cold run up and down my spine. It's the same ugly feeling I would often experience eight years ago when I first accompanied Andre in search of the mortal Jesus. I knew then, as I know now, that you don't undertake a task like that lightly. I also glance once more at the man reading the paper. He's staring at us in between glances of all the news that's fit to print.

I add, "I'm beginning to see why this wealthy Egyptian, whatever his name is, would be so interested in acquiring the bones. If they are proven to belong to the historical Jesus and if it's also proven that he was not crucified but lived to be an old man, it would inevitably show that the Koran is right, and the Bible is wrong."

"It would empower the Muslim Brotherhood and perhaps even factions like Al Qaeda like never before and it would effectively destroy the foundation upon which the Catholic Church has been established."

"How badly does this wealthy man want these bones?"

"Very badly. Enough to kidnap my husband and do so under Egyptian government authority."

I drink some more wine, look once more at the man. He's staring back at us. I pull a ten Euro note from my pocket, set it down onto the table, slide it under the empty glass.

"Let's go," I say under my breath.

"I haven't finished my wine," she says, looking up at me with those stunning pools.

"You're finished. We're not safe."

Gazing over her shoulder, she says, "That man is staring at us."

"There's a toilet in back. There's also a door that leads to the outside right beside it. Go now. I'll be right behind you."

She hesitates.

"Go. Now."

She gets up, walks to the rear of the bar.

I wait a full minute, then get up, grab my satchel, tossing the strap over my shoulder, and follow. I haven't yet reached the back door before I make out the heavy footsteps of a man running after me.

VINCENT ZANDRI

6

Anya is standing outside the door, her face a patina of panic and confusion.

The door is solid wood and locks from the inside but swings open onto the outside. Behind us exists a sort of gravel-covered, fenced-in no man's land which surrounds two small, blue plastic and metal dumpsters. One for refuse and another for recyclables. There's some concrete blocks and some two-by-fours set beside the dumpster.

The door opener rattles and begins to open. I push it shut with my arm and shoulder.

"Grab that two-by-four," I bark.

She does it.

I take hold of it with my left hand, jam one end into the gravel, then shove the other end under the brass closer. Pulling myself away from the door, I search for a way out of that small yard.

"This won't hold for more than a few seconds," I say, taking her hand.

"Where will we go?"

The man behind the door might have been following Anya for a while now. He might have followed her to my apartment earlier. In fact, it's very likely he followed her.

Behind us in the near distance, the ugly gray walls of the American University. A short chain link fence separates us from the school grounds.

"Your husband was teaching at the university. I assume they gave him the use of an office?"

"Yes," she says.

The man is pounding on the door, the two-by-four about to give way.

"Now's the time to show me."

She looks over her shoulder at the university building.

"This way," she says, and together we make our way over the fence and to the school.

The American University was built back in the

1960s. It is as uninteresting and sterile as the rest of Florence is beautiful, historic, and inspiring. Anya leads us through throngs of young students to a multi-storied concrete building marked "Science and Science Labs." Entry to the facility requires a key-code which you must punch into the keypad set right beside the metal and glass door.

"I don't know the code," Anya confesses.

"Just wait a moment," I say, shifting myself to the side of the door. "Someone will come along. In the meantime, keep an eye out for the man in black."

We wait for a beat or two, all the while, my eyes shifting from the door, to Anya, to the road behind me. When a man and a woman emerge from the door, the two of them engaged in deep academic conversation, I take hold of Anya's hand and slip us both inside.

"Slick," she says, as we enter the wide-open vestibule.

"What did you expect from a guy named Chase?" I say, smiling.

"Guess this means you're officially working for

me … Ren Man," she says as we approach the elevator.

"What the hell is Ren Man?"

"Short for Renaissance Man," she says. "That's a mouth full. Ren Man just rolls off the tongue a hell of a lot easier."

"You sure you want me to work for you?" I say. "You haven't heard my rates yet. What floor?"

"Second," she says. "Whatever the rates are, I'll pay them."

I hit the button containing a light-up arrow that points toward heaven.

"I'm beginning to like you, Mrs. Manion," I say, recalling how my dog Lu growled at her. "Even if I do suspect you're nothing but trouble."

"You have no idea, Ren Man," she says, smiling wryly as a bell chimes and the doors to the elevator slide open.

7

The office of Dr. Andre Manion is located midway down a brightly lit concrete corridor on the right-hand side. When I grip the opener, I find that it's locked. No surprise there. I step back from the door, look over one shoulder, then the other. Mounted to the exterior walls just inches below the concrete panel ceiling is a series of security cameras.

"Don't look now but we're being filmed," I point out.

Anya cocks her head over her shoulder.

"We are most definitely *not* being filmed," she says. "Those cameras are decoys meant to look like the place is secure. From what I'm told the American University constantly runs in the red."

"How do you know all this stuff if you and the missing hubby are split up?"

"First thing Detective Cipriani did when he found out my hubby, as you call him, was missing was to check the university security surveillance film. Stood to reason that if my husband simply walked out of here or worse, that he was kidnaped right out of his office, than it would be caught on film." She sighs. "Sadly, no such film exists since these cameras are for show only."

"What about a video of him leaving through the front door? Those cameras have got to be real."

She shakes her head.

"They're real enough," she says. "But no Andre to be seen on film."

"Then he was picked up off the street," I add. "Or maybe outside his apartment. Cipriani claims to have seen video of the professor at both the Florence and Cairo airports."

"Maybe. But what difference does it make at this point, Chase?"

She's got a point. This isn't a criminal investigation I'm running here. It's a rescue … More or less.

Reaching into the interior pocket on my worn leather bomber, I grab hold of a twenty-some-year-old Swiss Army knife. A gift from my dad before I disembarked for the first Gulf War back in '91. "Keep this where you can get at it quickly," he whispered into my ear before kissing my cheek and pressing his face against mine. I remember feeling the wetness of his tears as I stepped onto the Amtrak train that would take me to New York City and JFK, not wanting to look back into his big weeping eyes and risk seeing him like that. People die in wars. Young people. What if that was the last time we would ever see one another in this life?

Using the fingernail on my index finger, I pull out the metal pick option and slip it through the narrow hole located in the center of the closer. By pushing and twisting the pick, I feel the spring release on the closer's locking mechanism. With my free hand, I twist it counter-clockwise. With a pleasing metal-separating-from-metal snap, it opens.

"We're in," I say, opening the door wide.

I step in and Anya follows, closing the door

behind her.

"Lights," I say.

I hear her fumbling against the wall for a switch.

"Got it, Chase."

The room fills with bright white lamp light, thanks to the ceiling-mounted fixtures. The small, cramped, square office is filled with cardboard boxes that rest up against the wall to my right while to my left, numerous volumes occupy a steel bookshelf. Directly ahead of me, a metal desk is covered with scattered papers and photos.

I go to the desk and immediately see that maybe a half dozen eight-by-ten color glossies have been placed on top of a map. At closer inspection I can see that it's a map of Egypt. The Giza Plateau in particular. I slide the map out from under the pictures. It's covered in scribblings made in red Sharpie. So many lines, circles, and nonsensical doodles that I can't begin to make sense of it.

The photographs however leave nothing to interpretation. They are representations of the same white-on-black, photographic negative-like image.

"The Shroud of Turin," I whisper aloud.

"The Jesus burial cloth," Anya confirms, stepping beside me, so close I can feel her leather-covered shoulder rubbing up against my own. Her touch, no matter how slight, doesn't feel unpleasant. "Another one of my husband's obsessions."

I scan the photos which, too, are veined in red marker, as if Manion were searching for something he was convinced must be contained in the shroud, but not quite seeing it yet.

A map ... He was looking for a map. Or a blueprint ...

There are full body shots, head shots, arm and leg blow ups, even a zoom in on Christ's apparently blood-soaked hair.

"Question," I say, turning to Anya, hoping to squeeze a little more information out of her. "Why would a man concerned with looking for Christ's bones waste his time studying a crusade era forgery?"

She looks me in the eyes.

"It's true the shroud was finally proven beyond a

doubt that it dates back to 1352. That the pigment covering the cloth is not blood but paint. Vermillion and madder to be precise."

I was a bit struck by her obvious knowledge of the shroud. But then, I could only guess that she was able to pick up quite a lot about her husband's work by living with him for all those years.

"My question stands then. Why study it at all?"

"Because the shroud is more than a depiction of the body of Jesus as he was laid to rest in the tomb of Joseph of Arimathea immediately following the crucifixion. Andre was convinced that it was a giant map which was created in order to keep a precise and running record of the Jesus remains locations."

"Locations?" I ask. "As in the plural usage?"

"Yes, take it from a Freshman English Comp 101 teacher … Location*ssss*." She exaggerates the s at the end of "locations" making it sound like an extended Z.

I feel the light hairs on the back of my neck stand up at attention. Feel my blood begin to flow faster. So, Andre had been onto something all along. Eight years ago, whenever he'd bring up the subject of the shroud and its map-like possibilities, I would laugh and shrug it off as a nutty professor's overactive imagination. But now it appears his theory had some real validity to it.

She goes on, "For centuries people have been trying to make sense of the shroud, wishing and praying that it was the true cloth that wrapped Jesus's remains when he was pulled down from the cross. Proof of the mortal corpus *and* the divine resurrection incarnate. But, in all their zeal to confirm their faith, they never stopped for a second to consider that the shroud could actually be a guide in disguise. A way for the disciples, the bloodline of the disciples, and eventually, Holy Roman Catholic Church to keep track of the Jesus remains once he died."

"The cloth has been guarded over by Franciscan monks for centuries," I point out.

Anya nods.

She says, "The Vatican only allows limited testing every twenty years and even then, by a handful of

VINCENT ZANDRI

scientists they hand pick. For the rest of the time it's locked in an impenetrable vault. It's not even available for public display in its bullet-proof glass case expect for once every dozen years."

"Why give something that much protection if in essence it's just another 14th-century painting that might be hung in the Uffizi or the Louvre?"

"Precisely because the Vatican is aware of its true meaning as a map. A purpose and a meaning that would disprove the essence of Christianity."

"A purpose shrouded in the form of a fake image undergoing a false transformation." I burst out laughing. "A brilliant deception. The shroud is really the ultimate proof of Christ's mortality while at the same time masquerading as ultimate proof of his divinity. Talk about sheep in a wolf's clothing."

"Andre knows all this of course, and for years he's been begging the Vatican for close inspection of the shroud. It's part of the reason for his coming to Florence to teach within the proximity of the shroud in the first place. If he could get a serious look at it, he might discover not one map of the present whereabouts of the Jesus remains, but many maps detailing many different resting places. Andre firmly believed the bones were always on the move because they were always being hunted."

"Like now," I say. "He must have the map hidden somewhere."

"No," she says, once more shaking her head. "There's one major problem with my husband's map theory."

"And that is?"

"Whoever created the shroud wasn't foolish enough to simply draw detailed maps on the back and front of the Christ image. They hid them somewhere within the body itself. Existing photographs haven't been helping Andre find a precise location. They only offer tidbits of information. He needed to see the entire thing, face to face, in real-time."

"So, you're telling me Andre never actually uncovered a precise map." It's a question.

"Portions … Suggestions, but not a full map. A few lines and squiggles which were most definitely added in recent decades that, in this case, match up to specific locations in the Giza Plateau. While these recent map-like additions rule out previous locations or any other location for that matter, they still only spoke to Andre in generalizations." Raising up her hand, pointing at the map. "Thus, the photos and the map occupying the same desk."

"This tells me two things," I say. "First: Your husband only knows the *approximate* location of the burial site. And two: The people who kidnaped him have yet to steal the goods."

Wide-eyed, she nods.

"It might also mean that while the bones are still out there awaiting discovery, Andre is still alive."

"Yes, they will need him alive if they have any hope in unearthing their precious bony relics."

A bump on the office door. Not like a knock or a kick with the foot. More like someone, or something, trying to get in.

"Lock the door the door," I say.

Anya immediately jumps over to the door, locks the closer. That's when whoever is on the other side begins twisting the opener. Hard.

The man in black ...

"What do we do, Chase?"

I grab up the photos, stuff them in my satchel. I fold up the Giza Plateau map and stuff that too into the satchel. Giving the room a scan, I look for a way out.

"There's no windows," Anya says.

"I'm well aware of that," I say, looking for something, anything that will provide us quick egress.

Then I see the HVAC diffuser mounted to the top of the concrete block wall. Neither Anya nor myself are particularly big people. It might be a tight fit, but we just might be able to slide ourselves through the duct and down into the next room.

The person on the other side of the door is yanking on the closer, the door violently slapping against the metal frame. I pick up the desk chair, position it under the wall-mounted duct. Stepping onto the chair, I once more pull out the Swiss Army knife, this time fingering out the blade. Using the tip, I break off the heads of the old screws, then pull out the grill, dropping it to the floor.

"You first," I say, jumping down from the chair.

"Through there?"

"Yeah, this always works in the movies."

For the first time since I've known her, Anya truly smiles. She steps up onto the chair, sticks her head and shoulders into the duct.

"A little help please," she says.

I place one hand on her firm butt while wrapping my right arm around her legs.

"Pleasures all mine," I say, heaving.

"For a Ren Man, you're a real pig, Chase Baker," she says, before disappearing into the darkness.

8

I'm right behind her.

I drop down into the next room onto my black booted feet just as I make out the sound of Manion's office door being kicked in. We're standing in the dark inside someone's office. An office that appears to be empty, if not for an odor. Not a foul odor but a pleasant one. Aftershave maybe. Like Old Spice. Stuff my old man used to splash on his face before church on Sunday. I'm picturing the face of my old man when the body hits me like I've somehow stepped in front of a speeding truck. I go tumbling back against the wall.

"Chase," Anya screams.

"Find a light switch," I shout.

The man who tackled me led with his shoulder. The classic football tackle. He might have even bruised a rib. But he's not quick in retreating. I grab him in a headlock with my left arm while with my right, pull my automatic from its shoulder holster. I press the business end of the pistol against his skull.

"Don't shoot," comes a voice. The voice of an older man. He speaks English, but the accent is most definitely German.

I release him.

The overhead light comes on revealing my attacker. He's a short, gray-haired and bearded man dressed sloppily in an old wool blazer and corduroy pants. Most definitely a professor. He's even got a plastic pocket protector filled with pens and pencils plus a translucent six-inch ruler.

"I thought you were a burglar," he says, panting. "Or, perhaps, a rapist."

"You've got some spunk, Einstein, I'll give you that. We're the good guys. The bad guys are on the other side of this wall. Think you can call security for us?"

His eyes light up. He glances at my gun.

"I haven't had this much fun since I earned my

PhD in Physics forty years ago," he smiles.

"We're going to leave now," I say, crossing the office and joining Anya at the door.

"Go, go," the professor insists, picking up the phone on his desk, punching in a number. "I'm calling security. In the meantime, if they come through that vent, I'll be waiting for them." He raises up his free arm and makes a muscle under his jacket sleeve. Like I said, he's got some spunk.

"Sorry for the intrusion," I say.

"No worries. You made my day."

He begins speaking into the phone in Italian. I take hold of the door opener, slowly twist the knob, pull the door open, poke my head outside into the hall. I look both ways for a man dressed entirely in black.

"All clear," I say. "We'll take the stairs."

"Roger that, Chase."

"Roger that?"

Holding her hand, we step out into the hall, and take it double-time all the way to the stairwell.

Down on the first floor, we head back out into the

street.

People surround us on all sides. Students mostly, carrying books, canvases, sketchpads, knapsacks. Always moving about in pairs or groups. They stare at us with curiosity and perhaps even a little fear as they pass.

I grab Anya by the shoulders.

"We need to get back to my apartment while our tail is still busy upstairs with security. After that we'll have to find another place to hold up. The apartment isn't safe anymore now that I know you're being followed."

"I'm sorry. I just had no way of knowing."

"Don't be sorry. Goes with the territory. Sad thing is, that man probably isn't the only one watching you." Removing my hands. "Let's move."

"I'm right on your ass," she smiles.

"Now who's the pig, Anya Manion?" I say.

We run.

Continue Chase's adventure with your copy of The Shroud

Key

ABOUT THE AUTHOR

Winner of the 2015 PWA Shamus Award and the 2015 ITW Thriller Award for Best Original Paperback Novel, Vincent Zandri is the NEW YORK TIMES, USA TODAY, and AMAZON NO. 1 Overall bestselling author of more than 30 novels including THE REMAINS, MOONLIGHT WEEPS, EVERYTHING BURNS, and ORCHARD GROVE. An MFA in Writing graduate of Vermont College, Zandri's work is translated in the Dutch, Russian, French, Italian, and Japanese. Recently, Zandri was the subject of a major feature by the New York Times. He has also made appearances on Bloomberg TV and FOX news. In December 2014, Suspense Magazine named Zandri's, THE SHROUD KEY, as one of the Best Books of 2014. A freelance photo-journalist and the author of the popular "lit blog," The Vincent Zandri Vox, Zandri has written for Living Ready Magazine, RT, New York Newsday, Hudson Valley Magazine, The Times Union (Albany), Game & Fish Magazine, and many more. He lives in New York and Florence, Italy. For more go to WWW.VINCENTZANDRI.COM

VINCENT ZANDRI

YOUNG CHASE BAKER AND THE CROSS OF THE LAST CRUSADE

Vincent Zandri © copyright 2018

Bear Media 2017

4 Orchard Grove, Albany, NY 12204

http://www.vincentzandri.com

Cover design by Elder Lemon Art

Editing by of Plot2Published Editing

Formatting by Wit & Whimsy Designs

Author Photo by Jessica Painter

Published in the United States of America

The author is represented by Sam Hiyate of The Rights Factory.

Made in the USA
Middletown, DE
20 May 2020

95523007R00198